There was ...
a chance to ...

He certainly ha...
denied loving him. Even if he had to abduct
her and tie her to a chair he would make
her listen. She looked so distant, and he felt
completely lost. He could see he was losing
her.

'Please, Maddy. Tell me what to say to make
it better,' he said, his arms aching to hold her.
'I've never felt this way before. Never. And
it's because of you. Loving you makes me
want things I've never wanted before.'

Madeline swallowed a lump of emotion. His
voice was husky with passion. The plea in his
voice unmistakable. He sounded genuine, and
despite the dictates of her sensible brain her
heart was flowering, his earlier declaration of
love and his admission that he wanted to have
babies with her like welcome rain nourishing
fragile petals.

But at the same time her brain urged retreat.
How could she put her heart out there again?
She'd taken a risk with him, and his heat
and his passion had warmed her all the way
through and it had been fantastic while it had
lasted. But could she trust him…?

As a twelve-year-old, **Amy Andrews** used to sneak off with her mother's romance novels and devour every page. She was the type of kid who daydreamed a lot and carried a cast of thousands around in her head, and from quite an early age she knew that it was her destiny to write. So, in between her duties as wife and mother, her paid job as Paediatric Intensive Care Nurse and her compulsive habit to volunteer, she did just that! Amy lives in Brisbane's beautiful Samford Valley, with her very wonderful and patient husband, two gorgeous kids, a couple of black Labradors and six chooks.

Recent titles by the same author:

AN UNEXPECTED PROPOSAL

BY
AMY ANDREWS

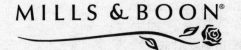

MILLS & BOON®

First published in Great Britain 2007
Paperback edition 2007
Harlequin Mills & Boon Limited,
Eton House, 18-24 Paradise Road, Richmond, Surrey TW9 1SR

© Amy Andrews 2007

ISBN-13: 978 0 263 85225 7
ISBN-10: 0 263 85225 3

Set in Times Roman 10½ on 12¼ pt
03-0307-50323

Printed and bound in Spain
by Litografía Rosés, S.A., Barcelona

AN UNEXPECTED
PROPOSAL

To Vicki Williams, homeopath, dedicated professional.
Many thanks for your time and expertise.

CHAPTER ONE

MADELINE HARRINGTON was grateful for the air-conditioning in her car as she pulled up at the roadworks. There was heavy earthmoving machinery blocking the way and as the heat rose in visible waves off the black tar of the road she'd never been more pleased to have an indoor job. The worker holding the stop sign looked hot and sweaty, his skin an unhealthy weathered brown. Skin cancer just waiting to happen, she mused absently.

It was hard to believe, watching Brisbane shimmer in the afternoon sun, that she'd been in the throes of a British winter only twenty-four hours ago. Jackets and gloves and woollen hats. As she'd flown out of Heathrow the temperature had just managed to struggle into positive figures. If London had been a fridge, Brisbane felt like a furnace!

She yawned and shut her eyes briefly as the overwhelming fatigue of jet lag took hold. She sighed as it gathered her into its folds but fought her way out again a minute later. Her eyes felt like they had sand embedded in the lids and she rubbed at them to ease the grittiness. The road blockage didn't look like it was going to clear any time soon and she sighed impatiently. She wanted a shower. She wanted her bed.

Her gaze wandered to the neighbourhood skate park where teenagers rode their skateboards up and down the curved cement walls. The doctor in her saw all the horrible possibilities but the uncoordinated female admired their skill and lack of fear.

A man entered her line of vision, expertly negotiating the bumps and ramps and shooting up off the wall, his skateboard staying miraculously attached to his feet even in mid-air, and landing again like he was riding a wave instead of unforgiving concrete. He was at least twenty years older than the other riders but somehow managed not to look ridiculous despite the age difference.

He was wearing a raggedy pair of cut-off denim shorts and nothing else. His chest was magnificent, tanned, the abdominal muscles well defined—cut, wasn't that what it was called these days? He pirouetted perfectly, one end of the board in the air, the other grounded, and her eyes were drawn downwards to his powerful quads that flexed and strained to maintain perfect balance.

She could see the hairs covering his legs were dark brown even from this distance. They matched his colouring. His head, too, was covered with brown hair, short around the back and sides and longer on top. *Why isn't he wearing a helmet? Macho idiot.* A smattering of the same covered his pecs and narrowed to a fine trail that disappeared behind the waistband of his shorts.

He looked like the stereotypical bronzed Aussie, at home in the outdoors, kicking a footy or surfing. Except today his choice of wave was concrete instead of water. Maybe he was some kind of adrenaline junkie—any wave would do?

The thought horrified her almost as much as it fascinated her. How would it be to spend your life bumming around skate parks? Or the beach? No responsibilities. No worries. No patients to see. No lives to be responsible for. No beepers. No mobile phones.

Looking at him made her…restless. A feeling that something was seriously missing from her life reared its ugly head and was magnified by the stranger's utter joy in the adrenaline-charged thrill.

He appeared to be with a little boy who looked about six or seven. His son? There were definite similarities between the two. The boy looked at him with total admiration and the man ruffled his hair as he helped him on his skateboard. He stood back as the boy performed a trick and clapped loudly as he successfully completed it. *At least he's wearing a helmet.* The man lifted the boy up on his shoulders and spun him around. The little boy held on and laughed, his head thrown back, the sunshine accentuating his exhilaration.

Madeline felt a weird pull low down in her gut. The man had dimples. He was gorgeous! Pure male. One hundred per cent testosterone. She felt her body responding to his magnetism. The boy obviously loved him and strangely enough that made him even more attractive.

Oh, God! She must be tired. Since when had macho he-men been her type? Spoken for he-men at that? She glanced back at the roadworks, suddenly desperate to get away from this inexplicable transient attraction, but the red stop sign was still stubbornly facing her way. She glanced back at skater boy and found herself wondering what it would be like to be with a man like him.

Despite the unemployed look, there was a presence about him that reached across the fifty-odd metres that separated them. He looked like he knew what he was doing. What he wanted and where he was going. He looked dominant and in command. He laughed again as he jumped back on his board and she recognised something else about him. He looked like he knew how to have fun. To laugh at the world and himself. He looked like he knew how to kiss. How to please. How to pleasure.

She shivered and reached forward to turn the air-con down. *Kiss? Pleasure?* Where had that come from? OK, it had been a while. It had been seven weeks since she and her fiancé had split up, and several months more since they'd last been intimate. But hell, that had never really been the focus of their relationship anyway and re-establishing the practice had taken up all her time and energy over the last two years. She hadn't had time for carnal thoughts.

Neither of them had. They'd barely seen each other for months, with her work and his long shifts at the hospital and studying for his exams. Him calling the engagement off in the middle of it all had been just one more thing on her plate. She'd been confused when he'd said he needed time apart. How much more apart did he want? But she doubted it would be permanent—a decade of history was hard to walk away from for ever.

Skater boy laughed again and oozed sex appeal all over the park. It brought her temporarily out-of-order relationship with Simon into sharp contrast. Frankly, she couldn't remember the last time, if ever, just looking at Simon had made her think sexual thoughts.

She shook her head. Jet lag—that was it. It was responsible for these uncharacteristic thoughts. Sex and sexual urges had never ruled her life. She'd been thrown one too many curve balls to be a free-loving kind of girl. For goodness' sake! She was a thirty-year-old doctor, she'd seen more naked men in her life than she'd had hot dinners—why should looking at barely dressed skater boy have an effect? Why did his chest and his thighs and his laugh make her want things she'd never wanted before?

A car horn blasted behind her and she looked back to the road to see the sign had been turned to the yellow 'slow' side and she accelerated away quickly, grateful for the respite from her jumbled jet-lagged thoughts. She caught a glimpse of the man again in her rear-view mirror and felt the feeling of discontent he had stirred intensify. Damn him. Her life was just fine.

Just. Fine.

Madeline pulled up outside work a few hours later. She'd unpacked. She'd had a shower. She felt slightly revived. But the fog of fatigue still clung to her and she'd known she'd had to get out of the house before she'd succumbed to her bed and the seductive lure of sleep.

It was way too early to go to bed despite her exhaustion. If she went now she'd be awake at three in the morning with no hope of going back to sleep. So a quick catch-up trip into work late on a quiet Saturday afternoon was the perfect diversion.

She noticed the next-door shop, which had been empty when she'd left, was in the process of a fit-out. A painter was admiring his handiwork, putting the finishing touches to the signage on the glass sliding door.

'Dr Marcus Hunt,' it read. 'Natural Therapist.'

Madeline stared at it for a few moments, repeating it over and over in her head until her sluggish brain computed the full implications. She felt the slow burn of rising anger.

'Over my dead body!'

There was nothing quite like anger to wake you up. She

felt it white and hot and burning in her gut. She felt more than awake, she felt alive again. The fog cleared from her brain and the weariness that was deep within her bones dissipated in an instant.

How many patients had she 'fixed up' after they'd seen alternative medicine characters? People who had let their conditions and diseases run out of control while some charlatan had used voodoo or a spell book and given them false hope? And then there was Abby.

She'd see about this! She brushed abruptly past the painter, slid back the door and entered the room. She blinked, removing her sunglasses as her eyes adjusted to the dim light in stark contrast to the glare of a summer's afternoon in the Sunshine State. The chemical smell of paint assaulted her nostrils as she quickly scanned the room littered with boxes and painters trestles.

'I'm sorry, we're not open for business until next week.' A deep, masculine voice drifted towards her from somewhere beyond the clutter of the immediate surroundings.

It resonated around the room and Madeline felt goosebumps break out on her arms despite the stuffiness of the room. His voice made her think of the guy at the skate park and she gave herself a mental shake.

The man entered from a doorway to the right and leant lazily against the jamb, filling the space easily. She almost did a double-take as skater boy smiled at her and Madeline was pinned to the spot by his laughing blue eyes and boyish dimples.

He was dressed this time. Well, more dressed anyway. He wore a white long-sleeved shirt, completely unbuttoned, revealing that perfectly muscled abdomen. The impulse to touch him, run her fingers down the dark trail of chest hair and watch his abdominal muscles twitch beneath her nails was shocking.

His face was rugged, with a square jaw covered in light stubble. His dimples should have looked ridiculous on anyone older than five but they didn't. They added to the alluring mix of pure man, giving him a shot of angelic boy.

In his right hand he held a well-used paintbrush and she thought absently that she'd been wrong about his employment status. He did have a job. A painter, or decorator, or something similar. He had some flecks of paint in his hair and the desire to touch them was compelling.

She couldn't help but compare him to Simon. Physically they weren't too dissimilar. Her ex-fiancé was a little shorter, a little less bulky, a little paler and his chest hair a little sparser. But there was something intangible about this man, something quite magnetic that frankly Simon just didn't have.

Simon's face was pleasant to look at, with a ready smile that put you at ease and oozed nice. Skater boy's was sexy with a wicked smile that put you on edge and made you forget nice. Simon was your average good-looking guy. There was absolutely nothing average about this man. And in their whole ten years as a couple Simon had never made her body hum like it was right now.

Madeline frowned, confused by her uncharacteristic thoughts. Labourers were not her type. Buff wasn't her type. Men that knew their way around skateboards weren't her type. Men with children weren't her type. What the hell was happening to her?

'May I help you?'

His voice was rich and deep and barely contained his obvious amusement at her appraisal. She was standing a few metres away but Madeline could feel the caress of the air currents, disturbed by his voice, swaying seductively over her. It was as if he had physically touched her.

She blinked at him blankly, trying to remember why she was there. His amused gaze eventually worked its way into her consciousness and she made an effort to pull herself together. So, the man had a nice body. She'd come to talk to the naturopath, not to ogle the removalist or the decorator or whoever in the hell this man was.

'Ah…no. I came to talk to Dr Hunt, but it appears he's not here…so I'll let you get back to your…duties.'

Marcus smothered a smile, suppressing the urge to throw back his head and laugh out loud. Put in your place, Marcus, old boy! The woman had just looked him over, summed him up and dismissed him as nothing in about thirty seconds flat! What a snob, he thought. What a sexy, beautiful snob.

She was tall and her head was crowned with the most magnificent red hair he'd ever seen. It was curly and looked slightly wild despite her efforts to tame it into a neat bundle at the back of her head. He had a sudden vision of it spread over his chest and he blinked.

Her emerald-green eyes sparkled above high cheekbones and two luscious lips. Kissable lips. Very kissable lips.

Her serious, obviously expensive suit did nothing to hide her fantastic figure. He felt his loins stir as he speculated on the bits of her long legs that were hidden by her skirt. She looked prim and proper and he was hit by the urge to get her dirty and messy. It was powerful, bordering on primitive.

She looked tired but there was an undercurrent, a vibe of tension around her that was almost palpable. Like a fully wound spring ready to unfurl at a second's notice. He'd never met anyone so uptight in his life. A large diamond flashed on the ring finger of her left hand. Surely someone getting regular sex couldn't be this tense?

'*I'm* Dr Marcus Hunt,' he stated, burying his left hand deep into his shorts pocket.

Madeline watched the movement hypnotically, until she became aware that she was staring at a particular part of his anatomy that she shouldn't be staring at. She dragged her eyes away, shocked at herself. She could see that he found her amusing. His grin, barely suppressed, added a sparkle to those blue, blue eyes.

'*You're* Dr Hunt?' she enquired with just the right amount of mingled sarcasm and disbelief. She had to get back some control here.

'Yes.' He swapped the paintbrush to his left hand, wiped his right on his denim-covered buttock and offered it to her.

She ignored it. Her rudeness seemed to amuse him even further and Madeline got the impression that nothing fazed Marcus Hunt.

'And you are?'

'Madeline Harrington. *Dr* Madeline Harrington.'

'Ah…from next door.' He smiled. 'We'll be neighbours, then.' The thought, despite the bling on her hand, was immensely appealing.

'Ah, no…I don't think so,' she stated with just the right amount of disdain.

'Oh?' he queried, not particularly worried. 'Problem?'

'Two, actually. One…' Madeline counted on her hand '…I object, most strenuously, to you using the title of Doctor. Naturopaths or any other alternative medicine nuts are not permitted to call themselves doctors.'

'They can if they hold a medical degree,' he stated matter-of-factly. 'And I'm a homeopath, actually.'

'You're…you're a *real* doctor?' Madeline spluttered in disbelief.

He threw back his head and laughed at the frank incredulity obvious on her face.

The long column of his neck was exposed to her view and, despite her embarrassment, an errant brain cell dared her to lick it.

'Is that so hard to believe?'

'Quite frankly, yes,' Madeline admitted. He didn't look like any kind of doctor she had ever known. Her father had been a doctor, his two nearing-retirement partners were doctors. Simon was a doctor! Those men were what doctors looked like.

'I believe there was a second…?' Marcus prompted after some time had elapsed and Madeline hadn't continued.

She made a supreme effort to drag her eyes away from his mouth and concentrate on the conversation.

'Yes. Secondly…' she cleared her throat, her chin jutting determinedly '…it will be a cold day in hell before I will allow you to practise this…quackery, this medieval…mumbo-jumbo, right next door to our practice. My partners and I will not legitimise this hocus-pocus by allowing you premises next to ours.'

Marcus stared intently at Madeline Harrington, listening carefully as she laid down the law. Two red spots of colour stained her cheeks and there was a breathy quality, almost a tremble, making her voice husky. He wondered what it would be like to have her breath trembling against his skin. His loins stirred again and he had to remind himself she was not on the market.

'And just how do you propose to stop me, Maddy?'

She opened her mouth to lay down exactly how she

intended to stop him and stopped abruptly at his casual familiarity. No one, but no one had called her that since Abby.
Sorrow and pain lanced through her as an image of her
younger sister formed in her mind. Why did it still have the
power to take her breath away?

'The name is Madeline,' she snapped.

'Maybe. But I think I'll call you Maddy anyway,' he stated,
and enjoyed the glitter he caused in her emerald depths.

'You won't be getting the chance, Dr Hunt. You're being
evicted first thing Monday.'

'I have a lease, Maddy.'

Madeline laughed coldly even as her insides melted at the
way he said her name. Almost a sigh. A purr. 'My partners
and I *own* this building, Dr Hunt. Once they discover that a
quack has set up shop next door, you won't last five minutes.
Not even your magic wand will be able to help you. Why not
leave graciously now? Go perform your witchcraft elsewhere.'

Madeline glowed triumphantly, having placed her trump
card on the table. He smiled back at her, obviously uncon-
cerned.

'Why stop at eviction, Maddy? Why not just burn me at
the stake and be done with it?' he enquired softly.

'Don't tempt me.'

Oh, she tempted him all right. 'What are you afraid of?
Have you forgotten that Hippocrates was a homoeopath?
Surely this world is big enough for both conventional and al-
ternative medicine?'

'Not in this street it isn't.' Madeline turned on her heel,
head high, and made for the door.

He chuckled. 'See you, Maddy.'

She shivered despite the blast of invading heat.

'Count on it,' she muttered, and stepped into the street.

* * *

Madeline breathed in great refreshing gulps as she walked the short distance next door to the GP surgery. She was quaking inside at the confrontation with Marcus Hunt and confused at the nagging sense of longing still crashing around inside her from when she had first spied him on his skateboard.

She let herself through the front gate of the inner-city terrace house that had been given a recent facelift, as had all the terraces in the area. The practice had been here for almost all of Madeline's life, her father having bought the row of five terraces before she'd been born and setting up with two other partners. The practice now took up two of the terraces, then there was the soon-to-be-empty-again one next door and the last two were leased by solicitors.

She looked at the gold lettering on the wooden door— Dr Blakely, Dr Baxter, Dr Harrington and Dr Wishart. Strangely, today she didn't feel the pride seeing her name in gold lettering usually engendered. She felt...disconnected. Unfulfilled.

She shook her head to clear the vague feeling of disquiet. Madeline had never wanted to do anything else. Most of the people that she'd been through med school with had been horrified at her lack of ambition. They'd been keen to specialise in the more glamorous areas of medicine. But she had grown up seeing the difference a good general practitioner could make to their patients' lives and had never considered anything else. And after her father's death she had grown even more determined to continue his legacy.

She pushed the door open. There was twenty minutes before closing.

'Madeline! Oh, my God,' squealed an excited Veronica from behind the front desk. The receptionist jumped from her chair and enveloped Madeline in an enthusiastic hug.

Veronica was one of the changes that Madeline had made since starting at the practice. Reasons for dwindling patient numbers had been multi-factorial, the new twenty-four-hour health centre in the next block being one but an aging reception staff not helping either. Veronica was twenty-five and a total godsend. She was bright and perky with a sparkly personality. The patients adored her.

'Fine,' Madeline responded distractedly. Not even Veronica's enthusiasm could curb her indefinable restlessness. 'Who's on today? George, Andrew or Tom?' Madeline asked, looking around at the empty waiting room.

'George. He's at a house call.'

George Blakely had been her father's partner since the dawn of the practice. He and his wife Mary had also taken Madeline and Abby under their wing when their parents had died within a year of each other in Madeline's final year of high school.

Andrew Baxter had also been one of the founding partners. Thomas Wishart was a newer edition, a thirty-three-year-old father of four, brought in by Madeline a year ago. He was an excellent practitioner who Madeline had first met at med school. They had desperately needed new blood to bring in new clients and Thomas, who lived locally, had been perfect.

Both George and Andrew would be retiring in the next five years so it was important to put strategies in place for that eventuality. Thomas had been an excellent start. The practice was building back up again and Madeline hoped that it would be thriving when George and Andrew hung up their stethoscopes.

'Quiet day?' Madeline asked.

'Forget that!' said Veronica, her blue eyes sparkling merrily, 'tell me all the gossip. I want to know everything!'

'I went to an international general practitioners' symposium, Veronica. No gossip to tell.'

Veronica rolled her eyes. 'In London, Madeline, London! Don't tell me you didn't take my advice?'

Madeline smiled. 'About the rebound sex?'

Veronica nodded her head vigorously. 'Those English lads love Aussie girls.'

'Ah, it's not really me, Veronica.'

'Well, of course it's not,' she said exasperatedly. 'That's the point. Simon dumps you just before a six-week overseas working holiday. It's perfect for rebound sex. Anonymity. Perfect.'

Madeline smiled at Veronica's grab-life-by-the-balls attitude and envied the younger woman. She herself was more tiptoe through life cautiously. One-night stands, rebound sex...she'd been with one guy for ten years. And, besides, their split was just temporary.

'I didn't really fancy anyone,' she said lamely as Veronica continued to look at her expectantly. Now, if Marcus Hunt had been there...

'Madeline,' Veronica sighed.

'Hey, no one offered either,' she said defensively.

'I don't reckon that helped,' said Veronica, tapping Madeline's ring with the end of her pen.

Madeline looked down at the two-carat diamond. It had been part of her hand for four years, and even if it was really over between them, she wasn't ready to take it off yet. And truth was, it did keep men away. If she counted Simon, that was four people she'd loved and lost, and she wasn't sure she would be capable of ever loving again. She felt emotionally frigid. Her heart buried in a block of ice.

She glanced at her watch. It was five. 'Why don't you go

home? It's time. I'm going to do a bit of catching up, I'll lock up on my way out.'

'OK, I get it, I get it. Mind my own business,' Veronica grumbled good-naturedly as she gathered her stuff. She gave Madeline a quick peck on the cheek and left.

Alone, Madeline walked around the surgery, absently re-familiarising herself with the tastefully decorated waiting area. She checked the appointment book and whistled out loud, recognising quite a few of her regulars. It was going to be a busy Tuesday! Her colleagues had insisted she didn't start work again until then, to fully recover from her jet lag.

Madeline felt the odd restlessness again and found it difficult to concentrate on the book. She yawned—she was tired but it was still too early for bed. She wandered into her office and sat in her chair. She picked up the various drug company 'toys' she kept on her desk to amuse children and opened her drawers, checking she had plenty of prescription pads and stationery.

The checks done, she sat back in her ergonomically designed black leather swivel chair and her tired mind drifted to Marcus Hunt. She saw the flecks of paint in his hair and heard his wicked laugh, and her nipples hardened at the image of his sheer masculine beauty. She'd never met a man who'd had such an instantaneous effect on her. Marcus Hunt was potent. Marcus Hunt was lethal.

Madeline's gaze fell on the framed photo of Simon. Something else she hadn't been able to bring herself to dispose of just yet. She remembered Veronica's pursed disapproving lips. It was all right for her. She'd spent her teens and twenties having a good time, experimenting with men and life, secure in the arms of a loving family. Madeline had spent them reeling from one tragedy to another while trying to study hard and be there for Abby, too. Simon had stuck by her side through all of it.

She traced her fingers over his face. So he wasn't skater boy but he had a nice smile and despite everything she still loved him. They'd been together for ever—since they'd been twenty. You couldn't just wipe that love out overnight. And she'd be damned if she'd let some inexplicable attraction to a bit of rough derail her conviction that the split with Simon was just temporary.

She heard the bell ding over the door and was pleased at the distraction. She thought it would probably be George back from his house call so she was surprised to see young Brett Sanders looking as white as a ghost, supporting his very grey, very sweaty mother.

Madeline hurried over. 'Mrs Sanders, what's wrong?' she demanded, quickly assessing the woman's cool, clammy skin, breathlessness and racing pulse.

'It's her indigestion,' said Brett. 'I wanted to take her to the hospital but she said she was fine and that you were closer. But she got worse in the car…' He trailed off, his voice cracking with fear and unshed tears.

'It's OK,' Madeline soothed, sitting Mrs Sanders down next to the emergency trolley near the front desk. It was basic, holding just oxygen, an ambu-bag, some adrenaline mini-jets and a portable defib unit. She quickly assembled a face mask and placed it on her patient's face, cranking up the oxygen. She hoped it wasn't too little too late. Mrs Sanders was in a lot of pain and it was extending down her left arm.

'Brett, go and ring the ambulance on the phone at the desk. Triple zero,' Even at seventeen, people in a panic could forget the number that had been drummed into them since they could talk. And Brett Sanders was about as panicked as she'd ever seen anyone.

'Tell them that your mum is having a heart attack. OK, Brett? Do you understand?'

He looked at Madeline, alarmed, and she thought he was about to cry. 'Brett.' Madeline shook him. 'I can't leave your mother. You must do it now. You've done so well. I need you to do this.' Her voice was calm but firm.

He got up and made the call, while Madeline took Mrs Sanders's blood pressure. Suddenly, the woman let out a pained moan, clutched at her chest and lost consciousness. Madeline knew immediately without having to feel for a carotid pulse that the woman was in cardiac arrest. With Brett's help she dragged the obese Mrs Sanders onto the floor, rolled her on her side and cleared her airway.

'Brett, run next door. There is a doctor there called Dr Hunt—get him. Go now, Brett—now.' Madeline knew from experience that CPR was much easier with two people. She just hoped he'd be able to see past their earlier confrontation. The youth took one look at his mother and fled.

Madeline dragged the recently purchased semi-automatic external defibrillator off the trolley, switched it on and followed the electronic voice prompts. She ripped open Mrs Sanders's blouse, buttons flying everywhere, cut open her bra with scissors from the trolley and slapped the two defib pads in the right positions on her chest.

While the machine analysed her patient's heart rhythm, Madeline assembled the mask-bag apparatus and hooked it up to the oxygen to deliver mechanical breaths to Mrs Sanders as soon as the machine had analysed the heat rhythm.

'Shock not recommended,' the electronic voice announced. 'Commence CPR.'

Madeline was in the middle of chest compressions when Marcus and Brett came through the door.

'What happened?' he demanded, shirt flapping wide.

'Fourteen, fifteen,' Madeline counted out loud with each downward compression of the sternum. She passed him the bag-mask and was grateful that he expertly took over the respirations, holding the mask and the patient's jaw with the practised ease of an anaesthetist.

'Myocardial infarction. She's arrested. The ambulance is on its way.'

They worked together as a team. Marcus gave one breath to Madeline's five compressions, stopping every two minutes for the defib to analyse the rhythm again.

'Shock recommended,' the voice said after nearly ten minutes.

Madeline almost cheered. They'd gone from an unshockable rhythm to one the defib deemed it could help. Had she moved from asystole into VF? Were they making real headway with their CPR?

Madeline checked they were well clear of Mrs Sanders's body before she pushed the shock button.

'Brett,' she said, 'why don't you go and wait for the ambulance outside? They'll be here soon.' The poor kid had seen enough today and was barely holding it all together. He didn't need to see how his mother's body would jump as the current arced through her chest.

'I don't want to leave her.' The boy's voice cracked with emotion he was desperately trying to keep in check.

'Brett,' Marcus said calmly, 'we have everything under control here.' He gave a reassuring smile. 'You can be a bigger help by greeting the ambulance and guiding them to us.'

Brett nodded miserably and left reluctantly.

'Stand clear,' said Madeline in a loud voice as they both backed away from the patient, making sure no part of them was touching Mrs Sanders in any way.

Madeline hit the green 'deliver shock' button and they both watched as the patient's chest bucked with the electricity. The machine told them to wait as it reanalysed.

'We need IV access,' Madeline said, slightly puffed from the exertion of depressing the patient's sternum. Her arms were beginning to ache.

'Shock not recommended,' the defib pronounced.

'Intubation gear, too,' said Marcus, as he resumed his position at Mrs Sanders's head.

She admired his skill but found herself wishing he'd do up his buttons. 'What? No eye of toad or wing of bat, Dr Hunt? No magic wand?' she taunted unreasonably, going back to her compressions. It was bitchy and uncalled for, given his willingness to help after she had called him a quack, but puh-lease! How could she even be thinking about his barely dressed body at such a time?

'Too late for that now, Maddy,' he stated, his lips tightening. Her gibe might have been amusing at another time but he too was way more distracted than he should have been by how her skirt had ridden up, exposing a generous length of thigh, and the way the silk of her blouse pulled tautly, sliding seductively over her pert breasts with each downward compression. There was a time and a place and this was definitely not it!

Madeline heard the sirens wailing somewhere close by and breathed a sigh of relief. Locked in this battle with Marcus to save Mrs Sanders's life seemed deeply intimate and she was pleased that other health-care professionals would soon join them and break the connection.

The two ambulance officers were there within the minute and Madeline explained what she knew and the four of them worked together. One of the ambulance team worked on intravenous access while Madeline and Marcus continued CPR. The other drew up first-line drugs.

'We need to intubate,' said Marcus when the machine recommended no shock again.

The officer handed him a laryngoscope and Marcus inserted the cold heavy metal into the patient's mouth as he manoeuvred her head with his other hand. The light on the instrument shone down her throat and Marcus angled it around slightly until he could visualise the white vocal cords.

'Size eight endotracheal tube, please.'

Marcus skilfully inserted the plastic airway into the trachea and removed the mask from the bag-mask apparatus, connecting the bag to the top of the tube and squeezing oxygenated air into the lungs. The paramedic tied the tube in place.

The machine reanalysed again and everyone moved back as it recommended a shock and Madeline pushed the green button. They moved back in and Marcus felt for a pulse.

'Got one,' he said.

There was no time for congratulations. 'Let's load her and go,' said the paramedic who had established the intravenous access. They swapped the defibs for one of theirs, which had a full-screen cardiac monitor attached, and Madeline helped load their patient onto the trolley as Marcus continued to administer breaths.

Madeline noted the tachycardia, relieved that they had

got Mrs Sanders back, but she was having runs of VT and Madeline knew that her condition was still critical and unstable. They had her ready for transport quickly and Madeline put her arm around Brett who was silent and pale, obviously shocked by everything that had just happened.

'Come on, son,' Marcus said gently, passing over the bag to the paramedic. 'You can ride up front.' Brett nodded absently, following his stretchered mother like a zombie.

'I'd like to ride in the back with her—is that all right?' Madeline asked the paramedics, who gave her a nod. If she arrested again, another pair of hands would be helpful.

'I'll follow in my car,' said Marcus.

She turned to face him and took an abrupt step back, not realising how close behind her he was.

'There's no need,' she said, trying not to sound ungrateful. After all, she couldn't have done it without him. Now the immediate emergency was over, the ebb of the adrenaline that had surged through her system was making her nauseous. Combined with her jet lag, she was shaking badly.

He put his hands gently on her shoulders and frowned at their trembling. 'Are you OK?' he asked, applying slight pressure to her shoulders.

She looked into his face and then wished she hadn't. She felt absurdly close to tears. She didn't want this man to be kind to her. She wanted him and the unsettling feelings she felt when she was near him to go away.

'I'm fine.' She shrugged her shoulders and his hands fell away.

Marcus lifted his hand and tucked a stray strand of hair behind her ear, which had loosened from the tight knot at the nape of her neck. Madeline pulled back as the urge to lay her head against his chest took hold.

'Dr Harrington,' one of the paramedics called.

'Coming,' she replied, and stepped away from Marcus on shaky legs.

CHAPTER TWO

MADELINE was sitting in the family waiting area with Brett
when Marcus finally tracked her down. On their arrival the
hospital staff had efficiently taken over. After briefing them,
Madeline had left to call Mr Sanders. She hated that part the
most. Talking to shocked families in grave situations always
made her feel helpless.

She was feeling really weary now, staring blankly at the
opposite wall, her eyes gritty again. Marcus pushed a
steaming cup of coffee towards her face. She blinked, staring
at him, unseeing at first until her body pulsed betrayingly and
recognition dawned. Overwhelming tiredness made her irritable.

'I told you there was no need to come,' she said, ignoring
the coffee. Didn't he have a child to get back to?

'Take it, Maddy,' he ordered in a soft voice which nonethe-
less brooked no argument. The pungent aroma of coffee hit
her and her stomach growled. Madeline realised she hadn't
eaten since breakfast on the plane. She took the polystyrene
cup.

He handed Brett a cold can of soft drink and sat down
beside her. They drank in silence, Madeline desperately
trying to quell the frisson of awareness just sitting next to

Marcus was causing. Their arms occasionally brushed and she was awake again. Fully, completely awake.

Pull yourself together, she lectured herself. He is unavailable. So are you, or you will be again soon anyway. And you're going to squash this man like an ant on Monday—you don't want to be lusting after him as you're giving him his marching orders. The thought kept her focussed and a smile curved across her full mouth and glittered in the emerald depths of her eyes.

She imagined the look on his face as she handed him the notice of eviction. The fantasy was marred by a sudden pang of guilt. They may not see eye to eye on treatment methodologies but he was an actual doctor and obviously very skilled, and had helped her tonight without question, despite her previous hostile threats.

'Plotting my demise, Maddy?'

His low growl in her ear caused a riot of sensations to surge through her. Startled that he could so accurately read her thoughts, she turned to face him, composing her features to disguise her inner turmoil. 'How did you guess?' she parried lightly.

'Maddy, Maddy.' He laughed and stroked the dark stubble on his jaw. 'Don't ever play poker.'

Madeline followed the caress intently, sidetracked by sudden wanton thoughts of his stubble brushing against her skin. Her nipples hardened and as she watched him his eyes widened and his hand stilled at her blatant arousal.

She stared for an age, caught in his intense blue gaze. The bustle of hospital life continued around them, oblivious to the sexual energy arcing between them.

'Dr Harrington.'

A young nurse interrupted. Madeline blinked and looked at her in a slightly disorientated fashion. 'Y-yes?'

'Mrs Sanders has just gone up to Intensive Care.'

'Oh,' said Madeline, pulling herself together, 'Thanks, I'll go right up.'

The nurse's attention, however, had strayed to Marcus. She was smiling at him, an invitation in her eyes. Marcus winked at her and Madeline rolled her eyes. Thank goodness she'd never been a slave to her hormones. How did people get things done? Stay focussed? Function?

She left him to it, taking Brett up to see his mother and waiting with him until his father arrived, leaving shortly after. She was surprised to see Marcus lounging at the nurses' desk, waiting for her, but was unsurprised to hear the tinkle of laughter as two more nurses fell under the skater boy's charm.

'I'll give you a lift home,' he said, straightening as she approached.

'I'll catch a taxi,' she threw over her shoulder as she walked past him.

'Don't be silly, Maddy,' he said, in a voice that made her feel like a disobedient child. 'You look exhausted. Do you know how long it's going to take to get a taxi on a Saturday evening?'

She stopped walking and sighed. He was right and she was tired, so very tired. What could it hurt? She nodded her assent. He raised his eyebrows at her, obviously not having expected such easy capitulation, but she was just too exhausted to care.

A few minutes later Madeline eyed the fire-engine red MG convertible doubtfully. '*This* is yours?'

'Yes,' he smiled lazily.

'Hocus-pocus pays, huh?' she gibed.

'What did you expect me to drive?'

She looked him up and down. He was still in the same

clothes—buttoned this time. She could see the paint in his hair and remembered him flying up off the concrete wall, his skateboard attached to his feet. 'Something old and beat up,' she said.

He threw back his head and laughed—a rich, throaty noise that weakened her knees. '*You* are a shrew,' he stated. 'Get in, Maddy.'

She obeyed meekly, fearing that her knees wouldn't support her for much longer. She sank into the well-worn soft leather of the bucket seat.

'Not much room for a child seat in here, Dr Hunt.'

He laughed again. 'The name is Marcus.'

'Maybe…but I'm going to call you Dr Hunt,' she mimicked his earlier words and he laughed again.

'*Touché*, Maddy. *Touché*.'

They rode with the top down and, apart from Madeline giving him the directions to her house, they drove in silence. The steady purr of the engine and the caress of the warm night air against her skin lulled Madeline to sleep.

Marcus took the opportunity to study her and felt a stupid little flutter somewhere in the vicinity of his heart. She was utterly gorgeous. Completely intriguing. The diamond on her finger mocked him and he almost sighed out loud. Pity. He lived by a strict code—no attached women, no matter how much his body insisted.

He pulled the car up outside her apartment block in the valley and switched off the engine. He didn't want to wake her but felt compelled to touch her at the same time.

'Maddy,' he said quietly, lightly stroking her cheek. She wiggled and murmured something unintelligible. 'Maddy,' he said, louder this time, and watched with regret as she opened her eyes. She sat up abruptly and Marcus's hand fell away.

'I'm sorry,' she said, embarrassed. 'I didn't mean to fall asleep.'

He shrugged. 'You were tired.'

They were quite close in the car and even in the dim light Madeline knew that something was happening inside her that had never happened with Simon. Marcus dominated the small space—his blatant sexuality too big for such close confines. This wouldn't do at all.

Oh, God! She was so confused. She needed a sleep! She was losing control of the situation completely. He rode a skateboard. He had a child. OK, that didn't mean he was married but he had responsibilities.

She cleared her throat. 'Anyway…thank you…for before. After the way I carried on I'm surprised you came.'

He shrugged. 'I would never ignore a medical emergency. Some things are bigger than petty differences.'

'Still, I think I owe you an apology.'

'Accepted,' he said, half bowing in the small space. 'Does this mean my imminent eviction is not on the cards?'

'It means seeing that you are a *real* doctor and you came to my aid and gave me a lift home, I guess I can tolerate you. But I'm a sceptic through and through, Dr Hunt. It'll take more than good CPR technique to convince me.'

He laughed. 'Ah, a challenge. I do so like a challenge.'

She shivered at the intimate promise in his words. This was crazy—he had a child and she was still wearing her engagement ring. She needed to put this conversation back onto even ground. 'I'd better go, I'm keeping you from your family.'

'Well, that would be difficult given I don't have any.'

Her heart did a crazy leap. 'Oh, I'm sorry, I saw you earlier today in the skate park with a little boy. I thought…'

She had seen him earlier? Interesting… 'He was my child? No. He's my nephew. My sister lives here in Brisbane and Connor's a mad keen skater. I promised I'd take him to the park on the weekend. Not married. Not in a relationship. No kids.'

He smiled at her and she thought, Free agent. No wife or girlfriend. And no child. 'I'm sorry. You seemed really close, I just automatically assumed…'

'Yeah, I guess we're pretty close. He's a great kid.'

'How old is he?'

'Six. When Nell, my sister, moved to Brisbane for her work I decided to follow. Connor's father took off when he was a baby and I know what it's like to grow up without a father.'

'What happened to your dad?' she asked, curious despite telling herself not to be.

'He and my mum divorced when I was five. He was kind of absent really. He married again and sort of forgot about us for large periods of time.'

'So now you're Connor's father figure?'

He laughed. 'Let's just say stable male role model.'

She wrinkled her nose. 'Ah, a man afraid of the F word. How unusual.'

He grinned. 'I'm not afraid. I just prefer being an uncle. I like being fun Uncle Marcus. But he's pretty full on. I'm glad when I can hand him back. I like my life a little too much to tie myself down to something like that permanently.'

'You make it sound like a death sentence,' she chided.

'Let's just say—once bitten, twice shy.'

So there was something in his past. 'Ouch,' she joked. 'Sounds painful.'

He shuddered, thinking about it. 'It was.'

Madeline yawned despite her interest being piqued. The weariness had returned with gusto. 'I'd better go. Thanks for the ride.'

He captured her gaze and the wrong kind of ride came to mind. Trying desperately to evict it from his brain, he cleared his throat. 'Any time,' he said.

Her hand stilled on the handle. Had she imagined the innuendo? She opened the door, exited the car and turned to face him. 'Goodbye, Dr Hunt,' she said, emphatically shutting the door.

His laughter followed her as she walked away on wobbly legs.

Madeline arrived at the hospital the next day just before lunch. She entered the main foyer, past the line of die hard smokers braving the midday sun, and into the blast of cool air. Madeline inhaled deeply, re-familiarising herself with the sterile smell found in hospitals the world over. She loved that smell and felt a pang of regret that she was no longer a part of the hospital system.

She made her way to the ICU only to discover her patient had stabilised and been moved to the coronary care unit. She spoke briefly to the registrar who had been caring for Mrs Sanders, and was told she had suffered a large inferior wall MI, evidenced not only on her ECG but by a massive rise in her cardiac enzymes.

Fortunately, with the swift administration of a thrombolytic agent they had managed to halt any further damage. Mrs Sanders's condition had stabilised overnight, with fewer and fewer ectopic beats, and they had been able to extubate her in the early hours of the morning.

Madeline was relieved as she made her way next door to

the coronary care unit. Mrs Sanders had five kids who needed her. Hopefully now she would start following medical advice and do something abut her diet and exercise. It was a drastic wake-up call but unfortunately her patient had been a heart attack waiting to happen for a long time—overweight, hypertensive, high cholesterol and a family history of heart disease.

Madeline smiled at Mrs Sanders, who was looking much better. She took her patient's hand as her eyes sought the cardiac monitor. A regular sinus rhythm blipped on the screen. The last blood pressure taken had been good and the oxygen saturation also displayed was excellent. No doubt this was helped by the prongs sitting inside Mrs Sanders's nose, blowing a steady supply of oxygen.

Mrs Sanders greeted Madeline warmly, thanking her profusely for saving her life.

'Nonsense,' Madeline said dismissively, blushing at the praise. 'I just did what anyone who had that knowledge would have done. Besides, I didn't do it all by myself.'

'Yes, Brett said that a nice male doctor helped, too.'

Madeline grimaced. That wasn't exactly how she would have described Marcus Hunt. Smug, yes. Sexy, yes. But nice…?

'Did I hear my name?' Marcus's deep voice behind her made Madeline jump.

'Maddy,' he said to her suddenly erect back as he entered the room.

Madeline, perched on her patient's bed, sat very still, awareness of Marcus stiffening her spine. He sauntered around the front of Madeline and sprawled himself in the low chair beside the bed. He offered Mrs Sanders the bunch of flowers he had.

Marcus introduced himself and proceeded to charm the socks off the middle-aged woman. Madeline sat rooted to the spot, unable to move and only vaguely aware of their conversation. Her eyes were irresistibly drawn to his powerful denim-clad legs. He was wearing one of those trendy T-shirts that looked like a toddler had scribbled on it and it clung to his biceps and chest wall perfectly. He laughed and it drew her gaze higher, to his mouth.

Marcus chose that moment to look at her with his strong, direct gaze. It broke her trance-like state and she looked away hastily, heat suffusing her face. I have to get out of here, she thought. I can't think straight around this damned man.

'Well, I think I'll be off now.' Madeline broke into the conversation with an unsteady voice and made a great show of gathering her things.

Mrs Sanders protested but Madeline could see how even the short visit had taken it out of her patient.

'Yes,' said Marcus, rising. 'I'd better be off, too.'

'Oh, please,' said Madeline, panicking slightly, not wanting to spend any longer in his company than she had to. 'Don't leave on my account, you've only just arrived. Stay. I'm sure Mrs Sanders would love the company.'

'No, no,' Marcus assured her. 'I don't think we should tire her out.'

'Yes, I am a little weary.' Mrs Sanders finally admitted the truth.

'Righto, we'll be off, then,' said Marcus, covering the older woman's hands with his own. 'If there is ever anything I can do for you, Mrs Sanders, please, don't hesitate.' He pulled a business card out of his back pocket and placed it on her bedside table.

Madeline stared at him, gobsmacked! She fumed silently as she stalked out of the unit. OK, she'd made up her mind to tolerate him but how dared he try and poach her patient?

Once they had pushed through the swinging doors and were out in the corridor, Madeline let fly.

'What the hell was that?' she demanded.

'Shh, Maddy…it's a hospital.' He wagged his finger at her playfully.

He looked so fresh and vital and she still felt tired and irritable. She wasn't in the mood for his teasing. 'I don't give a damn,' she snarled.

'Maddy!' He feigned a shocked expression.

'How *dare* you try and steal one of my patients? How…how…unethical! You're not doing a very good job of convincing me of your professionalism,' she snapped, striding off.

He contemplated just ambling along behind her, because her annoyed strut in her snug three-quarter cargoes was very cute, but thought better of it. He caught her up.

'Conventional medicine doesn't seem to have done her much good.'

Madeline halted and whipped around, cheeks flushed and eyes glittering. 'Don't you dare preach to me, *Doctor*. You know nothing about this case. It just so happens that conventional methods only work if you follow your doctor's advice! Mrs Sanders is notoriously uncompliant.'

Madeline's chest heaved, a fact not missed by Marcus. But unfortunately she didn't give him that long to appreciate it before she stormed ahead again.

Madeline was dismayed to find that some idiot had parked her in. Her dismay grew to anger when she realised it was Marcus's MG. She gritted her teeth. She was going to need thousands of dollars' worth of dental work done in the not too distant future if this kept up!

She kicked one of his car's tyres out of pure pique and

leant impatiently against her boot, foot tapping. She watched his lazy swagger as he approached. Even his strut was sexy.

'I hope you're better at your hocus-pocus than you are at parking.'

He laughed and she shivered despite the thirty-degree day. 'Someone got out of bed on the wrong side. Look I'm sorry, OK? I think we got off on the wrong foot this morning.'

'Just shift your car, Dr Hunt. I have no desire to speak with you.' She just wanted to go. Get out of his radius. His presence was too unsettling.

'Maddy,' he said, coming nearer, 'I thought we'd called a truce last night? I'm really a great guy when you get to know me.'

He was too close for her sanity. She found it hard to remember to breathe around this man. He made her inexplicably want to throw caution to the wind and hop on the back of his skateboard and roll off into the sunset.

'Your car,' she repeated.

Marcus gave a frustrated sigh at her stonewalling. He'd never had to work this hard in his life. And it just made him more intrigued. More fascinated. More sorry about the diamond rock on Madeline Harrington's left hand.

He gave her a long, hard look then moved away from her. He put the key in his door and decided she looked just as good in profile. 'Why don't we go and have a coffee or something? Get to know each other a little?' he asked her.

'Are you still here?' she said, ignoring his question.

He laughed. 'OK, OK. I guess I'll see you later.'

'Don't hold your breath,' she replied, and was pleased with just the right amounts of indifference and ice she'd injected into her voice.

Marcus gunned the engine and gave her another confident

grin. 'It may be sooner than you think.' His laughter reached out and touched her even after he'd accelerated away.

The muscles of her neck ached and she didn't have to be a chiropractor to know the cause. Stress. Also known as Marcus Hunt. He made her wary. Tense. On guard. She massaged them one-handed as she drove out to George and Mary's acreage property for lunch.

Mary handed her a nice cold Chardonnay as soon as she arrived and they sat out on the back deck in squatters' chairs, looking out over the gorgeous mountain view. George joined them and she filled them in on London and the events of the previous day.

'So you've met Marcus,' George said.

Madeline rolled her eyes. 'Yes, I have. Did you know he was a homeopath when you leased the premises to him?'

'Of course,' he said.

'What were you thinking, George?'

He looked at her calmly. 'I thought you might have a problem with it.'

'I threatened to have him evicted,' she said bluntly.

Mary gasped and held her hand to her mouth. 'Oh, no, dear! I've invited him to lunch.'

'What?' demanded Madeline, staring at Mary like she'd just grown another head.

'He'll be here any time soon.'

Oh, great, she thought. Was it too late to leave? Then she became annoyed. Why should she have to? George and Mary had been nothing but wonderful since her parents had died and she hadn't seen them for six weeks.

'Why on earth would you threaten to evict him?' asked a shocked George.

'Because I expected you to be as outraged as me. I thought you'd been hoodwinked by the estate agents and were oblivious to the identity of the new leaseholder.'

'Why would you think that?'

'Oh, I don't know,' she said sarcastically. 'How about all the botched-up patients we've seen? How about Abby?'

George looked at Madeline over the top of his glasses. She looked so much like her father. But Paul Harrington's daughter had been through a lot over the years and it had made her much tougher than the gentle soul who had been his dearest friend. She had been emotionally guarded since high school and Simon breaking off the engagement had made her even more wary.

He sighed and took his glasses off. 'I know she's your sister and you know how much we cared for her, but Abby was a grown woman who made her own decisions about her health care, Madeline,' he reminded her gently. 'Yes, she was foolish but ultimately it was her choice who she consulted that day. You can't brand the entire industry because of a few bad eggs. Abby must also share some of that responsibility.'

Madeline knew he was right but Abby had paid such a high price for her stupidity. 'I know that. I'm just surprised that suddenly we appear to be endorsing this stuff,' Madeline said.

'Madeline,' George sighed, getting up and moving closer, 'Marcus is one of Melbourne's top people in alternative medicine. He's even worked with elite athletes, helping them find alternative medicines to treat their ailments because so much conventional stuff is on the banned list. We had him thoroughly checked out. He holds a bona fide medical degree. He's not some radical quack. Just a good doctor offering people choices based on sound medical and homoeopathic principles. The best of both worlds.'

She knew George was making sense but an image of Marcus's dimpled smile was stuck in her brain and she wanted it gone. 'Why wasn't I consulted?'

'You've been away for six weeks.'

'There are such things as telephones.'

'It wasn't a decision we made lightly, Madeline. We all discussed it and agreed that it would be good for the practice to promote holistic care. You're not the only one keen to make changes so we can attract new clients. You opened the box and you've really helped revive the practice, but we have ideas, too. So many people come in these days wanting alternatives to pills and intrusive medical procedures. At least we can refer them to someone with an impeccable reputation.'

'You mean you're actually going to refer patients to him?'

'If I feel it's warranted. If it's what they want—yes.' He shrugged.

'I don't know, George. It's one thing to tolerate him but to legitimise him by passing work his way is another thing entirely. You know we have to strive for best practice. And that has to be evidence-based.'

'Come on, Madeline, so much of modern medicine and pharmacology is based on old remedies.'

She nodded thoughtfully. 'Maybe. But that's the problem with all this alternative nonsense, isn't it? There's no written studies to back up their claims. If it isn't written somewhere, proven in some double-blind study somewhere, I don't think I'll be referring any of my patients.'

And she wanted as little to do with him as possible. There was something strange that happened inside her when she was around him. It was confusing and she didn't need it in her life. As it was, she was going to have sit through lunch with him. Him and his blue eyes and wicked dimples.

'You will be nice to him, won't you, dear?' said Mary.

Manners were very important to Mary. 'Of course, Mary. I'm always polite,' she said, trying to keep the irritation out of her voice. Since when had she ever not done the right thing?

The phone rang, interrupting their conversation. Madeline hoped it was Marcus cancelling lunch but when George didn't come back from answering it she assumed it was for him. Mary went to check on lunch, ordering Madeline to stay where she was and relax.

Which she did. Despite the frisson of apprehension about Marcus, the combination of the heat and wine and jet lag and the quiet tranquillity of the Blakely residence had her eyelids growing heavy. Horses neighed and cows mooed and the smell of freshly cut grass filled her senses. I'll just shut my eyes for a second, she thought sleepily.

Madeline vaguely heard the chiming of the doorbell but was still lost in the nether world of sleep when Mary directed their guest outside. 'Madeline's out on the deck. I'll be there in a moment, Marcus, dear. George won't be long.'

Marcus strolled out, steeling himself for uptight Maddy, still annoyed at him about what had happened at the hospital. He almost did a double-take when Madeline's sleeping form came into view. She wasn't remotely uptight in slumber. Her hair was loose and her eyes were closed and her disapproving mouth was soft and her frown was gone. He suddenly knew how the prince in *Sleeping Beauty* must have felt.

She lay reclined in the chair, her long legs stretched out on the leg supports of the squatter's chair. A half-empty wineglass balanced on the broad arm. His eyes drifted to the steady rise and fall of her chest. She wore a jade-green T-shirt with a rounded neckline that clung to her female form.

The temperature outside suddenly got a lot hotter. Marcus felt his mouth go dry as the heat started to suffocate him. God! She was beautiful. He felt his groin stir and tighten. He sat at the table and watched her as she slept. This time he wasn't going to wake her, not when just looking at her gave him pleasure. He had no idea who the man was that Maddy had committed herself to but he was one lucky guy.

Madeline frowned slightly as an image of Marcus floated in front of her. His bare chest and dimples mocked her. She awoke with a start, disorientated, her subconscious trying to drag her back into the lingering folds of her dream.

Her unfocussed gaze came to rest on Marcus. He was staring at her and she frowned. The fog shrouding her brain, intensified by her out-of-sync body clock, couldn't compute the image in front of her. Was she still dreaming? Had she only dreamt that she'd woken up? Or was she dreaming that she was awake?

Marcus waited for the confusion to clear from her gaze. She was looking at him like he was an alien. Which was fine by him because when she finally did realise who he was she was going to be as mad as hell.

Madeline blinked rapidly a few times and rubbed her eyes. Yep—she was definitely awake. And Marcus was definitely sitting at the table, drinking a beer. Looking at her.

'Maddy.' He nodded. 'Long time, no see.'

Madeline felt vulnerable in her reclining position and struggled out of the chair. 'Madeline,' she grouched, annoyed that he'd showed up. 'The name is Madeline!'

'Do you need a hand?' he asked, amused at her attempts to get out of the chair.

She ignored him, finally rising to her feet and walking down to the far corner of the deck, wineglass in hand. He was dressed as he'd been at the hospital. His comment about seeing her sooner than she thought flashed back.

'You knew! You knew at the hospital you were coming here,' she accused.

'Mary invited me this morning. It seems she's rather keen for us to meet. Besides…I never refuse a home-cooked meal.'

Madeline was just about to retaliate when Mary came out to join them. 'Everything OK?' she asked.

Madeline could see Mary looking at the distance between the two of them and the little frown drawing her eyebrows together.

'Great,' said Madeline, and smiled enthusiastically.

'Marcus…' Mary wagged her finger at him '…you never said you and Madeline had already met.'

Madeline stared incredulously at sensible, level-headed Mary. She was practically flirting with the younger man, her cheeks a delicate pink.

'I confess.' He dazzled a brilliant smile in Mary's direction.

So it wasn't just her he had an effect on? Madeline suppressed the sudden urge to scream. 'Where's George?' she asked instead.

'Here I am,' he said, joining them, giving his wife a hug from behind. 'Let's eat!'

Mary was an excellent cook and Madeline was sure it tasted divine, but she found herself having to force down each mouthful. She was acutely conscious of Marcus and his witty chat. She could barely string two words together, which added to her irritation.

'So, Marcus,' Mary said, 'tell us a bit about yourself.'

Marcus told them a lot about his earlier life growing up in Melbourne and Madeline was interested despite telling herself she didn't care.

'I'm surprised a nice young man like you hasn't been snapped up with a couple of kids by now,' Mary pressed.

He laughed. 'Can you call thirty-five young?' he asked.

George snorted. 'You can when you're sixty.'

Madeline was just thinking how smoothly Marcus had avoided that question when she saw his smiling face grow serious.

'Actually, I was married once, a long time ago.'

Madeline stopped eating. His cryptic comments in the car the previous night now made some sense.

'Too young?' asked Mary.

'Something like that,' he said dismissively with a quick shrug of his shoulders.

'Do you still see her?' Mary asked.

'From time to time,' he said noncommittally, thinking about how stupid he and Tabitha had been the last time they'd caught up.

They ate a little more without speaking and then Mary said, 'Have you had much of a chance to do any sightseeing, Marcus?'

'Not really,' he admitted. 'I've been so busy since I arrived, setting up the practice, I haven't really been anywhere. I've found South Bank, I swim there most afternoons. Oh, and the local skate park.'

Yes, indeed he had, thought Madeline as she pushed her food around her plate. She thought back to when she had first seen him—had it only been yesterday?—shirtless, riding the concrete curves. His six-pack abs and his perfectly muscled quads returned in full Technicolor detail. If only she'd known then, sitting in her car at roadworks, that in less than twenty-four hours she'd actually be acquainted with skater boy, she might just have turned around and flown back to the UK.

She became aware that the other occupants of the table were staring at her expectantly. She shook her head. 'I'm sorry…what did you say?'

'I was just telling Marcus what a wonderful tour guide you are. You won't mind showing him some of the local sights on your day off tomorrow, will you?' Mary said.

Madeline blinked at her. Of course she minded! Was Mary not listening when she'd told her about the eviction threats? Was she insane? She groped around desperately for a way to wriggle out of it.

'Ah…well, actually, I was kind of planning on lazing in bed. This jet lag is a killer.'

Marcus thought about Maddy lazing in bed and nearly choked on his mouthful of food.

'Not all day, surely,' George interjected. 'Even half a day would be better than none.'

She looked from one to the other. She knew they prided themselves on making strangers welcome but this was ridiculous. Did they feel badly that Madeline had made a scene with him already and were trying to make amends?

Now it seemed they were conspiring together. She had an uneasy feeling and hoped they weren't trying to set her up. She wondered how shocked they'd be if she told them she'd rather be run over by a bus than spend a moment alone with Marcus.

'It's OK, George, Mary…Madeline obviously feels uncomfortable with the idea of being my tour guide. I'll see the sights another time.'

Madeline's back stiffened. She glared at him and his eyes

twinkled at her. He was making her look very spoilt and un-gracious and he knew it. The Blakelys placed a lot of value on good manners and hospitality and she owed them a lot. She'd be damned if she'd let him show her up in a bad light.

'OK,' she surrendered.

'Thank you, dear,' said Mary, her eyes twinkling.

George shot her a grateful smile and Madeline could see that it meant a lot to him.

'Why don't I pick you up?' suggested Marcus. 'What time?'

Madeline had no real interest in the details. She shrugged. 'One?'

'Looking forward to it,' he said softly.

Madeline looked into his blue eyes and wished she'd never met him. Suddenly she wanted out. She rose and busied herself with the dishes.

'We'll do this, dear. Why don't you go home? You still look very tired,' Mary said kindly.

Normally Madeline would have argued and insisted that she do the dishes but the invitation to leave was too tempting.

'Thanks, Mary.' She kissed her gratefully on the cheek. 'I really am bushed.'

'Will you be all right, driving home?' asked George.

'Of course.'

'I can give you a lift,' Marcus offered, standing quickly.

Mary clapped her hands. 'What a good—'

'No!' Madeline exclaimed loudly. Perhaps a little too loudly as her hosts looked at her somewhat startled.

Madeline shot Marcus a look that told him in no uncer-tain terms to back off.

'No,' Madeline repeated, not so loudly but with definite firmness. 'I'm not *that* tired. I'll be fine.'

Marcus smothered a smile. She made it sound like being in the car with him was a fate worse than death. He watched as she gathered her things and kissed the Blakelys goodbye.

'Don't bother to see me out. Stay with your guest,' she told George as he stood.

She bade Marcus a brief goodbye because it would have been impolite in front of George and Mary to poke her tongue out and kick him in the shins, which was her first instinct. He'd cornered her and he knew it. But she didn't have to like it.

'Till tomorrow,' he said.

Madeline stilled momentarily and their gazes locked. She felt a tremor of awareness slither up her back. There was something between them that scared the hell out of her. How did he make an innocent outing feel so carnal?

'Tomorrow.'

CHAPTER THREE

THE pounding was like jackhammers drilling into her brain, the noise echoing loudly and ricocheting off the bones of her skull. Madeline groaned and clutched at her temples. The pounding intensified.

Desperately trying to drag herself out of the clutches of sleep, Madeline tentatively opened her eyes. The tablets she had taken the previous afternoon for her approaching headache had left her feeling disorientated, as if there was soup where her brains should be.

The banging began again and Madeline realised that it was coming from the front door, not from the headache that still throbbed at her temples. But the noise jarred through her head, aggravating the thumping within.

Still disorientated, Madeline rolled out of bed, mumbling unintelligibly. The red digits of the alarm clock told her it was five past one. Afternoon or morning? Her deliberately darkened room let in no tell-tale signs of light. What day was it anyway?

She stumbled through the house, reaching the front door and grabbing desperately at the lock. She had to make the pounding stop.

'All right, all right,' she snapped as she wrenched open the door, 'Quit that awful racket.' The full glare of the midday sun assaulted her vision and she shielded her eyes as pain lanced her eye sockets.

Marcus Hunt stood there, slightly surprised by Madeline's dishevelled, almost wild appearance.

'You look awful.' His concern was mirrored in his blue eyes.

Actually, he thought, she looked pretty damn hot. Yes, she was obviously unwell but at this moment she looked wild, untamed. Her fiery red hair was loose and slightly mussed from the sleep he had obviously woken her from. He felt sure had Titian been alive today he would have killed to paint her hair.

She was wearing a plain grey T-shirt that moulded her breasts and grey cotton boy-leg knickers. He's never seen so much of her flesh and Marcus felt the denim of his jeans grow taut as a small fire ignited in his loins.

Hell, man! Pull yourself together, he admonished himself. She's unwell, for God's sake. The usual brilliant green glitter of her eyes had dulled to a lacklustre jade. He doubted that she would answer the door in next to nothing to anyone, *especially* him, had she been in her right mind.

Madeline stared at Marcus, trying to figure out what the hell he was doing here on her doorstep, but stopped when it became too painful. Her eyes hurt from the glare and not even his dazzling good looks eased the thumping.

'Thank you for your brutal honesty,' she snapped. 'Now go away.' Madeline swung the door closed but his quick reflexes caught it before it was half way shut. She sighed loudly and turned on her heel. She didn't care what he did, she was going back to bed.

Madeline made her way back to her room and collapsed on the bed, dragging the sheet up to cover her body.

'Maddy?' he called from the bedroom doorway.

She opened an eyelid and almost groaned out loud. 'Are you still here?'

'You're not well.'

What a brilliant deduction! 'Yeah, well, you're not helping.'

'Did you forget our date?'

Madeline sat up abruptly in bed, wincing as the sudden movement reverberated through her grey matter. 'Date?'

'You were going to show me the sights?'

'Oh, God.' She did groan this time. 'I'm sorry—I forgot.' The headache had obliterated everything.

'That's OK. We'll do the date another time.'

'It's not a date,' she said, not bothering to hide her irritation. 'I was being polite. I wouldn't date you if you were the only man on earth.' Pain knifed into her skull again and she lay down quickly as a wave of nausea hit.

Marcus would have laughed but when Madeline clutched her head and moaned and collapsed backwards, he realised she was in a bad way.

'Headache, Maddy?' he asked as he moved into the room and sat beside her on her bed.

'Madeline,' she corrected him through gritted teeth.

'When did it start?' he enquired. He reached for her arm and felt for her pulse.

Madeline flinched at the contact, adding a few more beats to her already racing heart. She would have moved away from him had she not been gripping her shirt so tightly to stop from vomiting right here in front of him.

Marcus noted the vice-like grip turning her knuckles white.

'Yesterday afternoon.'

'Is this a regular occurrence?'

She shook her head, finding his fingers at her pulse quite soothing. 'Once every few months.' She relaxed her grip on her shirt as the nausea subsided.

'What brings them on?'

'Stress,' she stated bluntly.

'And what's been stressing you lately?' he asked innocently.

Yeah, right! Like he didn't know! He was the main reason she had this wretched headache. If she hadn't spent hours worrying about this stupid outing— A fresh wave of nausea struck. She wriggled her hand away to stop her treacherous body betraying her. It was his fault she felt dreadful.

'You are kidding, right?' she said, opening one eye and fixing him with a glare.

Marcus smiled. He had given her the headache? Well, that was a first. He'd been known to cure them before…

'Have you always had them?'

'No, I got my first one about five years ago.' About? Who was she kidding? Madeline remembered it as if it were yesterday. The afternoon of Abby's funeral she'd been practically incapacitated.

'Was that a particularly stressful time then?'

She shut her eyes, not wanting him to know just how awful it had been. 'You could say that.'

Marcus watched as Madeline rolled onto her side, facing away from him. End of conversation. He rubbed his jaw absently as his gaze followed the slender curve of her back. In holistic medicine, knowing about stress triggers and what caused them was an important part of his diagnosis and treatment. But he wasn't going to find out at the moment and, whatever the deep-rooted cause, Madeline's debilitating symptoms were of more pressing concern.

Maybe if he cured it, her opinion of him and his job would improve? Maybe he would gain some ground? Why it was so important that he did he didn't want to analyse at the moment—he just knew she got to him. And he didn't like to see anyone suffer.

'Have you taken something for it?'

Madeline's eyes drifted open as his voice reached out and joined the hammering in her head.

'Several Mersyndol.'

No wonder she was acting spaced, he thought. No, that wouldn't do. A massage. That's what she needed. Nothing like a good massage to relieve stress and tension. Lavender. He needed some lavender and other essential oils to induce relaxation. He'd better get going. He had a lot to prove today.

'Maddy? I'm going to leave you now.'

'Hallelujah!' she muttered.

He laughed. 'Sorry to disappoint you…I'm coming back. I'm just going to get some stuff for your headache.'

'Don't bother, Marcus, I'm afraid I don't own a cauldron.'

Marcus laughed again. Even bedridden by a blinding headache, she could be as sharp as a tack. Would she ever miss an opportunity for a dig? 'No hocus-pocus, Maddy, I promise.'

Whatever, Madeline thought as she shut her eyes and drifted away on her Mersyndol cloud. The little white pills did lessen the severity quite a bit but she knew that they mainly worked by altering her perception of the pain, which wasn't quite the same as curing it. But it would run its twenty-four-hour course and the pills would help make it more bearable.

Marcus returned forty-five minutes later to find Madeline curled up in a foetal ball on the bed. 'Madeline,' he said quietly.

She opened her eyes and squeezed them shut again as she felt the mattress sink under his weight. He was back? She almost screamed, except she knew that would only hurt her head more. *Maybe if I lie very still he'll go away,* she thought. *Maybe he'll think I'm asleep.*

'Madeline,' he repeated, switching on the bedside lamp.

If her head hadn't felt like it was about to fall off her shoulders, she would have yelled at him to go. But she just wasn't capable of anything that excessive. She opened an eye and looked at him disparagingly.

Even in the dim light Marcus once again noted how dull her eyes were. Gone was the brilliant green of a highly polished emerald. Now they reminded him of the dull raw stone just plucked from the earth. He held up a bottle of oil that had just the right blend to restore their usual brilliance. 'I have the perfect thing for headaches.'

She eyed him dubiously. 'If six Mersyndol haven't helped, I doubt very much that what's in that bottle can. I'll pass.'

'Oh, ye of little faith,' he tutted.

'What is it? Do I have to snort it, swallow it or inject it?'

He laughed. 'None of the above. It's massage oil. I apply it. Roll on your tummy,' he ordered.

Even through her drug-induced, disorientated haze, Madeline had enough wits to know that she would be entering dangerous waters if she allowed him to do this. The strange pull she felt around him hadn't been obliterated by the migraine, just buried a little. And a massage in her bedroom, on her bed….

She stared at him and tried to fathom how he didn't seem worried about the intimacy of the situation. Was she the only one that felt the weird energy between them? The…thing…that she'd felt from the moment she'd seen him on the skateboard?

'I don't think that's a very good idea,' she said huskily.

'Come on, Maddy, I mixed a secret potion.' He grinned. 'I know you don't believe in any of this but at least give it a go. It works. Really it does.'

So she *was* the only one that felt it? He looked strictly professional. No indication that they were anything other than practitioner and client. Her head was too sore to try and figure it out. Thump, thump, thump. Her head pulsated with painful regularity. She doubted seriously whether a massage would help but…what if he was right?

'OK,' Madeline agreed, shifting gingerly onto her stomach.

'I'll look away while you take your shirt off,' he said. 'Use the sheet to cover up.'

Madeline raised herself on her elbows and looked back over her shoulder at him. 'I don't think so,' she said.

Marcus sighed in frustration. 'Don't be ridiculous. I need full access to your neck and shoulders. I can't give you a proper therapeutic massage through your shirt. I am one hundred per cent professional whether you think so or not. I don't come on to women under the guise of my work and I certainly don't come on to women who are engaged! Ever.'

Normally Madeline would have been mortified to have insulted anyone—she was just too polite. But the thought of him touching her was sending her hormones into chaotic overdrive. Marcus looked insulted that she had questioned his ethics but, seriously, the thought was as terrifying as it was irresistible.

He turned his back and she quickly divested herself of her shirt, pulling the sheet up around her, her feet sticking out either side.

'Ready,' she said.

Marcus turned back, still miffed that she would doubt his professional boundaries. Ok, this wasn't a doctor-patient relationship but there was a line you just didn't cross in these situations. He was perfectly capable of distinguishing between therapeutic and sexual and the two groups of women that each was appropriate for!

Madeline lay stiffly, her breathing ragged, waiting for the touch of his hands on her neck. She heard him rubbing the oil between his hands and her shoulders tensed, waiting for the glide of his fingers at the nape of her neck. So when he gently stroked her feet she almost leapt off the bed.

She felt like he had just plugged her into a power point. Energy arced through her, electrifying every cell in her body. Her body hummed with the intensity of a city grid as the life-force pulsed through her. How on earth was this going to help her headache?

'Relax, Maddy, it's OK,' he crooned quietly. 'I thought I'd start with a reflexology massage of your feet. Did you know there are certain pressure points on the soles of the feet that correspond to certain parts of the body?'

'No hocus-pocus, you promised,' she accused, her voice muffled from being buried in the pillow as she tried not to moan out loud.

He chuckled. 'Such a sceptic. OK—no attempts at conversion. Forget the science behind it. How about you just enjoy it because it feels fantastic?'

Well, she couldn't argue with him there, she admitted, biting her lip to stop herself audibly groaning as his deft fingers probed and rubbed her feet. He seemed to linger and concentrate on some areas, particularly her big toes, but wherever his fingers roamed they left devastation of cyclonic proportions on her equilibrium. He lavished equal attention

on both feet and although Madeline would never have
admitted it out loud, she could feel the intensity of the
migraine beginning to ebb.

He stopped after twenty minutes and Madeline stifled a
protest. It wouldn't do at all to have him think she actually
wanted him to continue. She dragged her scattered wits
together.

'Thank you, that was most kind,' she said in a small prim
voice, masking the inner turmoil he had created. She started
to move.

He chuckled and placed a stilling hand on a shapely calf.
'The best is yet to come.'

Madeline shook her head, alarmed that he was going to
wreak further havoc on her equilibrium. 'No, it's all right. I'm
feeling better now,' she said, turning her head to look over
her shoulder at him. 'I just need to sleep it off now.'

'Shh,' he whispered, placing two fingers against his lips.

Madeline's pupils dilated as she followed the movement
and the desire to have him touch her lips with his oily fingers
in the same manner and draw his fingers into her mouth and
taste the beautifully aromatic oil shocked her. She didn't
understand where such thoughts came from. Up until she had
met Marcus, she'd never felt so out of control of her body.

'Lie down, Maddy,' he ordered gently. Madeline
Harrington was quite a conundrum. Why did a beautiful, de-
sirable woman look so perplexed by a man's touch?

She obeyed quickly, the pounding in her head being
replaced by a deep, slow pounding in her chest. She stiffened
momentarily as she felt his hands in her hair but relaxed
when she realised he was gathering together the loose tendrils
and pushing them off her neck.

Marcus fought the urge to bury his face in her beautiful

locks. He could smell her shampoo as the scent wafted towards him. Frangipani and cinnamon. He was moving into dangerous territory. The look she had just given him had been heavy with desire and if he continued there was no way he could take the moral high ground and pretend the massage was still only therapeutic.

Madeline felt the oil on the heated flesh of her shoulders and was amazed it wasn't sizzling. She could hear his breathing as his fingers stroked gently through the liquid. Was she mistaken or was it as uneven as hers? She'd known the man for two days and had allowed him liberties that had taken Simon months to earn.

Lavender filled the air with its sweet fragrance. There were other fragrances as well that she couldn't place.

She cleared the huskiness from her throat. 'What's in the oil?' she asked. She prided herself on sounding almost normal. This was good. This was what she needed. A little conversation to distract her from the traitorous pulse of her body.

'Guess,' he said, and slowly ran two glistening fingers under her nose and along her top lip.

Madeline almost moaned out loud and the temptation to suck them inside her mouth was so real she ground her toes into the bed to stop herself.

She swallowed. 'Ah…lavender?' she said. 'And it smells a bit minty, too. But there's something else…I don't know.'

He chuckled. 'Very good. Lavender, peppermint and the other fragrance is melissa oil—it has a citrus aroma,' he said.

Madeline shut her eyes as Marcus's fingers probed the muscles of her shoulders and neck. He applied more oil and worked a little deeper and she bit her lip to stop herself from whimpering. 'And what do you use as a base oil?' she asked, desperate to convey normality.

'It depends,' he said massaging her neck. 'Lately I've been using grape-seed oil.'

She vaguely heard his answer. The effect of his touch was profound and she gave up trying to fight it. The strangest sensations were taking a grip on her body. Madeline felt all her tension ooze out of her pores. The longer he kneaded and caressed, the better her head felt. It wasn't long before the migraine had all but disappeared.

Heat unfurled along her nerves, melting her muscles and dissolving her bones. She felt weightless yet heavy at the same time. Her breasts ached and there was another ache, deep down low, and she pressed her thighs together to get some relief from the steady build-up of pressure.

Simon had never touched her like this. Therapeutically, sexually or otherwise. They'd been engaged for four years and together for ten and she couldn't remember the last time she'd been this hot under the collar. When had been the last time they'd been carried away on a wave of passion?

Looking back at their relationship, she had to admit it hadn't been just the last couple of frantic years when their intimacy had taken a nose-dive. It had never really been based on passion. They'd known each other since kindy and had just kind of fallen into a relationship at university without really realising it.

Simon lost his mother in the first year of med school and she'd been there for him. Having only just lost her own mother to breast cancer, she'd understood his devastation. So they'd started to hang out together and people had started to assume and it had been convenient for two busy med students to not have to worry too much about matters of the heart. And then when Abby had died five years later during her final exams, he'd become her rock.

But as Marcus's fingers continued to weave their magic down the length of her spine, Madeline had to wonder what the hell she'd been missing out on! Simon's touch, his kisses had never been like this. They had been nice rather than passionate, polite rather than magical. But that had been OK. What did that stuff really matter when you loved someone?

Actually, it had suited her. Secretly, deep down she'd always thought that her profound grief had rendered her incapable of grand passion. It had been hard to get in the mood when sex had seemed unimportant compared to the things she had already lost. But now, lying there as Marcus made her body hum and sing and come alive with a deft touch and a bit of oil, she knew she'd been wrong. She was sexual. She was a woman with a woman's needs. That sex mattered. A lot!

The thought depressed her. Here she was, nearly naked on her bed with a man she barely knew who was creating complete and utter havoc inside her, and there wasn't anyone she could turn to. What would Veronica say? *Turn over right now and let him massage your front.*

She bit her lip. She couldn't do it. It just wasn't her. But as she gave herself up to the kneading and the stroking and the rubbing, a blissful euphoria enveloped her, lulling her into a deep relaxing slumber. And a little piece of the ice around her heart started to thaw. Marcus had started a flame, a tiny spark of heat, and each rub of his fingers fanned it a little higher.

It took Marcus several minutes to realise that she had fallen asleep. He was way too busy concentrating on coaxing the deep knots of tension out of her neck and shoulders. Too busy pretending she was Mrs Furness—a rather large, sour lady who had made his professional life very unpleasant on the occasions that he had been unlucky enough to see her.

He figured if he could just keep picturing this awful woman he wouldn't be tempted to replace his hands with his mouth. He wouldn't lick and suck at her small earlobes, taunting him through the tumble of her glorious hair. He wouldn't kiss her neck and turn her over and show her passion that would make her forget all about her fiancé.

Because she was out of bounds. Way, way out of bounds.

The digital clock read five minutes to five when Madeline woke up. She felt slightly disorientated in the darkened room and rolled onto her back, sighing loudly.

Marcus came into her line of vision. He was sitting silently in one of the chairs from the lounge room, deeply engrossed in a book. His head snapped up at her movement.

'Marcus?' she asked, momentarily puzzled by his presence. Her migraine had gone but the all-too-familiar after-effects had taken its place. Her brain felt fuzzy, all her thought processes seemed jumbled and she felt totally sapped.

'Good evening, Maddy. Feeling better?'

His chirpy mood grated on her recovering nerves. Memories of the massage and her body's reaction to it swamped her. 'I feel fine, thank you. There was no need for you to stay,' she said. 'You may as well go now.'

She went to sit up and then remembered she was naked except for her knickers. She could feel a blush steal up her face and hoped that Marcus couldn't see it through the gloom. Now she was awake and the memories were flooding back, she was acutely embarrassed by the rather intimate nature of their afternoon.

'So I'm dismissed, am I?' he enquired, one black eyebrow rising slightly, an amused smile playing on his lips.

He made her sound churlish and she felt herself go redder still. 'I'm grateful,' she said, forcing the tremor from her voice. 'Really I am. But I don't need to be babysat.'

It was weird, talking to a fully clothed Marcus as the sheets slid seductively across her bare flesh, grazing her nipples and making her acutely aware of her state of undress. He was two metres away. In her bedroom. She didn't know what she was supposed to do or say.

'I'm not leaving until I'm sure you're going to be OK. Get up. Have a shower. I'll rustle us up something to eat.'

'I'm not hungry,' she said automatically, even though she was starving. She just wanted him as far away from her as possible.

'You need to eat something,' he said, and his voice was firm. 'And I think you at least owe me a meal.'

He was right. He'd arrived at her place expecting to have an afternoon on the town and instead had spent his time ministering to her. She opened her mouth to agree but he'd already left the room and she could hear him opening cupboards in the kitchen.

Marcus looked up when he heard Madeline shuffle into the kitchen ten minutes later. His welcoming smile slipped slightly as he took in her appearance. Baggy trackpants, baggy sweatshirt, fluffy pink slippers, hair tied back into a neat plait.

No shape. About as asexual as she could get. Marcus almost laughed out loud. He knew what she was trying to achieve but he didn't have to see it to know that underneath all that thick padding was a fantastic body. Not that long ago he'd had his hands all over it! She would look sexy in sack-cloth.

'Going for a jog?' he queried sardonically.

She ignored him. She felt back in control of her body and the situation again. 'Hmm, that smells wonderful. What is it?'

'Omelette,' he said, 'And it's ready. Let's eat.'

He had made himself at home in her kitchen, judging by the beautifully set table. Marcus placed a huge plate of steaming eggs in front of her, followed closely by a mound of buttered toast. Madeline's stomach growled ferociously as the odours made her mouth water.

They ate in silence. Madeline savoured the rich, mouth-watering flavour of the omelette. Marcus savoured her animated appreciation of his cooking. The shower had obviously done her the world of good, he thought. It had brought the colour back to her cheeks. She looked much better.

Marcus finished and pushed his plate away. He sat, arms folded, regarding her, expression blank. Madeline stopped, egg-laden fork paused halfway between the plate and her mouth. His stare was very unsettling.

Their gazes locked. Madeline's ears filled with the pounding of her heart. A slight vibration of the fork betrayed the frantic beat.

'What?'

'Nothing. Just watching.'

Madeline tried not to be self-conscious as she ate but found it too unnerving. 'Must you?' she asked impatiently, putting down her fork.

Marcus chuckled, a low deep noise, and Madeline breathed easier when he got up from the table. He prowled around the dining room, inspecting her framed photographs.

'This the ring-giver?' he asked.

Madeline looked up and saw him with Simon's photo. Her first instinct was to admit they were no longer engaged, but if looking at a photo of Simon served as a reminder to Marcus that she was spoken for, even if it was temporarily untrue, then she wasn't going to disabuse him. 'That's my fiancé, yes,' she said, hoping that a huge lightning bolt wouldn't crack open the ceiling and fry her where she sat.

Marcus stared at the other man for a while. 'So why isn't he here, looking after you?'

'He's a busy surgical registrar at the hospital. It's difficult to synchronise our schedules.' She shrugged, irritated by his subtle criticism. 'He has a lot on his plate.'

'Surely some things are more important,' Marcus said.

Madeline couldn't believe he was forcing her to defend a man who had dumped her! 'His shifts suck and he's got exams coming up. I'm not a child. I can look after myself.'

Yes, but sometimes it was nice to be looked after. Marcus shook his head at the framed photo. What an idiot, he thought, and thanked God he'd not been lured into the crazy world of speciality medicine! Who would choose their work over Maddy? Did the man not realise that she might not be there when he was finished forging a career? Beautiful women like Maddy needed to be appreciated and adored—not neglected!

'What?' she asked defensively, noticing Marcus's disparaging look. It seemed strange that another man was in her house, making himself at home, touching her stuff, looking at her pictures.

'Nothing,' he said, and put the frame down.

'No. There was something,' she insisted.

'Look, I've never met him and I'm sure he's doing a great job but…the guy is an idiot, Maddy.'

She blinked a few times, not quite believing that he had just said what he'd said. 'I beg your pardon? He finished top of the class. He won the university medal. He's no idiot.'

Marcus shook his head instead of following his first instinct, which was to shake her. 'Oh, I'm sure he's brilliant, Maddy. But, trust me, any man that can neglect you can't be all that smart.'

Madeline wanted to leap in and object, defend Simon, but Marcus's compliment stopped her in her tracks. She blushed and found herself wondering for a moment how it would feel to have someone so into you they couldn't even bear to leave your side.

He put the photo down, deciding that he'd never understand men like that or why Maddy thought it was acceptable.

'Your parents?' he asked, pointing at another picture. She nodded and he continued, 'I'm sorry. George said they're both dead.'

Madeline nodded again, touched by the genuine warmth and sympathy in his voice. He held her gaze for a moment before turning back to the photos.

'Who's this?' he asked.

He was holding a small silver frame displaying a picture of Abby and Madeline shortly before her sister's death. It was Madeline's favourite. They had spent the day out shopping together and had caught a movie. They'd been laughing about the light-hearted comedy when Simon had snapped the candid shot.

She felt the familiar sadness encroach. 'My sister.'

Oh, George hadn't mentioned a sister. They certainly didn't look alike. The younger woman was smaller and blonde. 'Does she live in Brisbane?' he asked.

'Not any more. She's dead,' Madeline said quietly, rising to take the photo away from him.

Marcus felt as if she had just socked him between the eyes as he passed it back. He reached out to put his hands on her shoulders as a gesture of comfort, but she flinched and stepped out of his reach.

'How long ago?'

'Five years.'

Ah. Now that explained a lot, especially the headaches. Until she had resolved all her grief Marcus suspected they would continue to plague her. 'What happened?'

'One of your lot killed her.'

The quiet statement exploded into the silence around them. She traced her sister's face with her index finger and Marcus shut his eyes against her anguish for a few moments and prepared himself for what he knew was going to be a really horrible story about some fly-by-night who had taken a young woman's life through his quackery.

'Let me guess, a snake-oil salesman from Chinatown? A voodoo priestess?' Marcus knew all about the seedier side of his chosen field and the unqualified people out there who pedalled cures for a fast buck.

'Psychic surgeon.'

'Oh, Maddy,' he whispered. He wanted to draw her into the circle of his arms and comfort her but she was standing stiffly, every body language cue she possessed telling him to back off. 'They're not holistic therapists. They're—'

'Quacks? Charlatans? Witches?' she said, feeling cold inside again as the same hopeless despair she had felt when her deathly ill sister had landed on her doorstep revisited. It had been too late to help her and she'd been unable to do anything as the life-force had slowly ebbed from her sister.

Marcus heard her pain and better understood her vehemence that first day. 'I'm not responsible for the entire industry, Maddy. There are unscrupulous practitioners on both sides of the fence.'

She held her sister's photo up to him. 'Save it,' she said.

The girl in the picture looked about twenty. 'Maddy—'

She held up her hand, indicating for him to stop. 'Look, I know I was harsh the other day and you're right—there are incompetents everywhere. But I'm a doctor. By my very nature I'm sceptical. However, as you've just cured my migraine, which even I have to admit is quite an amazing feat, I have to give you kudos for that. I'm not completely shut off to different ideas, Marcus, but I need to see the science. Show me the literature, the evidence, the replicated double-blind studies.'

'I agree, this is an area where my field of medicine is lacking. But I want to assure you that any practice I employ is evidence-based. Any time you want to see the literature, just ask.'

'Oh, I will,' she said, and sighed wearily, replacing the frame. 'You can count on it.'

He laughed and saw a small smile flit across her lips. She yawned and he realised how done in she looked. He knew how much migraines sapped energy levels so he shelved any further conversation.

'I'm going to go and leave you get back to bed,' he said, priding himself on how calm he sounded when the thought of her in bed set his heart pumping loudly.

Madeline nodded as a shiver prickled her skin. She daren't look at him in case he could read her very unladylike thoughts.

'Here,' he said, and held out a small tin.

She looked at the offering in his hand but made no effort to take it. 'What is it?' she asked sceptically.

He picked up her hand, opened her palm and placed the tin in it. 'Feverfew leaves,' he said. 'I know you're not a believer and I understand you have more reason than most to be suspicious of what I do, but if you take it regularly, as an infusion, it's great for migraine prophylaxis.'

She stared at the tin for a few seconds and looked up just in time to see him heading out the front door. She opened the lid and then slowly brought it up to her nose to sniff it. It didn't smell hideous—in fact, it was quite pleasant. It probably wouldn't hurt to give it a try.

Still, she suspected not seeing him ever again would be the best prophylaxis of all.

CHAPTER FOUR

MADELINE felt wonderful the next morning. The usual hangover she'd normally wake up with after a migraine was non-existent and she knew she had Marcus and his magic touch to thank for that. Even though it had been that touch responsible for the vivid erotic dreams that had weaved their way through the haze of her subconscious all night. She'd woken aroused, the spark now a furnace licking heat deep inside her, and she had to make a conscious effort to get her butt out of bed.

Luckily her first day back at work passed fairly quickly, for which she was grateful. The more work the less time she had to think about Marcus and how his touch had awoken a slumbering nymph. Quite how she was going to handle that she wasn't sure…

She was fully booked, her regulars more than pleased to see her. Madeline knew that if patients were ill enough, it hardly mattered who they saw, but it took a while to build up a relationship and a rapport with a doctor, and it was only natural to feel more comfortable around your own GP.

There wasn't anything too taxing for her first day. Just the usual array of aches and pains, mole checks, grizzly babies, requests for repeat scripts, several referrals, a couple of vac-cinations and a few pap smears.

Since Madeline had joined the practice the previous year she had introduced a lot of changes, particularly in the area of women's health. And it was paying dividends. They were attracting an increasing female clientele. Even a lot of the older ladies who didn't believe in female doctors now preferred Madeline to look after their 'women's business'.

She was immensely proud of this. She was pleased that the female clients of the practice, both old and new, had confidence in her. And that George and Andrew did, too. It hadn't been easy at times and they had made her work damn hard to prove herself, but she'd enjoyed the challenge and had reaped the rewards.

One of the reasons she had gone to the UK, apart from the symposium, had been to look at ways of incorporating a well women's clinic in the practice, something that focussed on proactive instead of reactive, and she dearly wanted to get a local support group for the growing numbers of teenage mothers up and running. Some of the UK models she had seen were very impressive.

She had lots of ideas and she was lucky that her father's old partners were open to suggestions. She had known them all her life and both were very dear to Madeline. It had been a dream come true that they had made room for her in the practice and she had nothing less than a full partnership in her sights.

But first she had to earn it. That took hard work and determination and fortunately she was blessed with an abundance of both. Her innovations were helping to rebuild a client base which had been dwindling, and Madeline was determined to forge a bright future for her father's beloved practice.

* * *

At about three o'clock, Constance Fullbright entered her office. Madeline had been dreading this visit all day. Although fifty-year-old Connie was a nice woman, she was the resident hypochondriac. She had been a patient of Andrew's for thirty years but he had eagerly passed her on to Madeline when Connie had decided that perhaps a female doctor was a better idea.

'Hello, Connie,' said Madeline.

'Oh, Dr Harrington! So good to have you back. This has been the longest six weeks of my life! Promise you'll never leave me like that again.'

Madeline smiled. 'I have to have a holiday some time.' She laughed.

'Oh, yes, I suppose,' the other woman said, lowering her hefty frame into the chair opposite Madeline. 'But, well, it's just not the same, seeing anyone else,' she complained. 'Andrew is a dear soul and he was my doctor for a long time but, well…it's just not the same as you, my dear.'

'Well, thank you, Connie. I'll take that as a compliment. What can I help you with today?' Madeline knew from experience that if you didn't keep Constance on track, the consultation would last for ever. She was lonely and loved a good gossip. But there was just never the time for that and particularly not today with still a good twenty patients left to see.

Madeline listened to her patient describe her latest medical problem. She wrote occasional notes in Connie's very thick chart. Madeline would have seen Connie at least once a week for the last two years. Sometimes twice. Over that time Madeline had investigated Connie for all number of things, including insomnia, heavy periods, mood swings, aching joints, diplopia, headaches, sore throats, fever and forgetfulness.

Connie had become a human pincushion but nothing had shown up on any of her tests other than what Madeline had always suspected, which was falling oestrogen levels, indicating Connie was going through menopause. As well as this there was Connie's obesity and lack of exercise. Madeline could see another Mrs Sanders waiting to happen. Or at least a case of diabetes. Maybe even a stroke.

Today, Connie was describing prolonged fatigue. Again, a classic change-of-life symptom. There were so many things that Madeline had spoken to Connie about to help her through a period in her life that a lot of women found daunting. From diet and exercise tips through to menopause support groups. But it had all fallen on deaf ears

Connie wasn't big on effort. She wanted a magic pill that could cure all her ills, real and imagined, and didn't involve too much of a demand on her. Unfortunately, Madeline knew that there was only so much modern medicine could do for menopause symptoms and the rest was up to the patient.

'I'm thinking I might see if a naturopath has any answers. What do you think, dear?'

Madeline prepared herself for her standard talk she usually gave patients who were thinking of dabbling in the alternative health field. She never said don't, even though every part of her wanted to. It was her job to guide her clients, give them the correct information and let them make up their own minds. But this was just one of those subjects she found hard to be objective about.

As Connie rabbited on and on and she waited for an appropriate place to get a word in, Madeline started to formulate a plan. Yes, she'd said she'd never refer to Marcus but...if the patient wanted a referral then...why not? Marcus had said she should give it a chance, and if Marcus could cure

Connie, well, she'd definitely need to rethink the whole alternative medicine field. A migraine would be a snap compared to Connie and her multiple problems. If he could make headway with her, she'd have to start believing in miracles!!

'Connie,' said Madeline, breaking into the monologue. 'How about I write you a referral to the new natural therapist who's opening next door? He's a homeopath. He doesn't open till tomorrow but I reckon I can get you an appointment first thing.'

'Could you? Oh, that would be marvellous.'

'I'll talk to him this afternoon. Veronica will ring you with the appointment time,' she said as she wrote out the referral letter on her personalised stationery.

She refrained from being unprofessional. Madeline knew full well that the majority of patients opened their letters and read them. But she smiled slightly as she thought about the endless possibilities. A hex on your house, Marcus, she thought as she signed the letter.

Marcus was locking up about five when he saw Madeline, briefcase in hand, coming out of her gate. She gave him a quick wave and walked away in the other direction. Perfect— he was heading that way, too. He grinned to himself at how prim she looked in her navy pinstripe suit, her hair tied in her regulation nape-knot, and wondered as he watched the sway of her hips whether she was wearing lacy lingerie beneath or the cotton underwear he had seen her in the previous day.

'Who's that, Uncle Marcus?'

The boyish voice of his nephew intruded on his fantasy. Marcus looked down at Connor, whom he'd picked up from school earlier and brought back to the practice as a favour to

Nell, who didn't knock off until six. He'd helped him with his homework and then Connor had helped him, unpacking boxes like he did it for a living. Of course, using the skate park as a carrot had helped.

'Her name's Maddy. She's a doctor next door.'

'Is she your girlfriend?'

Marcus laughed. Only in his dreams! 'No. Why?'

Connor shrugged. 'You were looking at her kind of funny,' he said. 'And she's really pretty.'

Marcus nodded. His nephew must have got that keen eye from him. 'Yes, Connor, that she is,' he said.

'Can I ride the board to the park?' Connor asked, throwing it down on the ground and pushing it backwards and forwards with a foot.

'OK, but stay close and don't go too fast. Remember you're going downhill slightly. If you break your arm your mother will kill me.' His nephew laughed at him as he did up the chin strap on his helmet and checked his knee and elbow pads. Yeah. Bulletproof.

Madeline had heard the skateboard approach and she hadn't needed to turn around to know it was Marcus. She was fast gaining a real sixth sense where he was concerned. She braced herself for his presence and found herself wishing he'd get thrown off on one of the many cracks in the aged footpath just to avoid having to look at him after last night. Honestly— a grown man riding a skateboard deserved to fall on his butt!

But the board swished straight past her and the boy riding it gave her a cheeky grin. He was familiar and she realised it was Marcus's nephew. When Marcus did catch her up a moment later, she jumped.

'How are you feeling today, Maddy?'

'Fine,' she said, not bothering to stop or even acknowledge

him as her heart thundered madly. She knew she should thank him again for his help but, given the way the night had ended and the things he had made her feel and the subsequent dreams, the less conversation about the previous day the better.

'Finished for the day?'

'Yup,' she said, again refusing to look at him.

'Can I walk with you?'

No, you can't. She shrugged. 'It's a public pavement. Your nephew?' she asked.

He nodded. 'Hey, Connor,' he called to the boy a few metres ahead of them. 'Come here and meet Maddy.'

Connor braked and with some fancy footwork flipped the board up into his hand and tucked it under his arm.

'Hi,' said Connor, as he approached.

'Connor, this is Maddy.'

'Hi,' said Madeline, gritting her teeth to not correct Marcus in front of the boy. He was very cute, his uniform shirt untucked, and Madeline got a glimpse of Marcus at six.

'That's a pretty name,' he said.

Madeline blinked. She always forgot how candid children could be. 'Actually, my full name is Madeline.'

Connor thought for a bit. 'Oh. Maddy is much prettier.'

Yep, definitely a chip off the old block, thought Marcus as he chuckled and then ruffled his nephew's hair.

Madeline shot him a disparaging look. 'Is your uncle teaching you how to ride?' she asked Connor.

'Nah, I already know how to do that. He's teaching me to do tricks. Oops.' He clapped a hand over his mouth and looked stricken. 'I wasn't supposed to tell anyone.'

'Don't worry, Connor. Your secret is safe with me,' she said, and smiled at him reassuringly.

He looked at his uncle uncertainly. 'Sorry, Uncle Marcus.'

Marcus laughed. 'It's OK, mate. Go on, get on your board.'

They watched Connor ride ahead a bit. Madeline turned to Marcus and pinned him with a 'please, explain' look. 'Let me guess, he's not supposed to tell his mother, right?'

'He wants to learn and I'm teaching him. He's a boy, he needs to be wild. Nell's a little too protective.'

Madeline shook her head at him and strode off, briskly this time, but he caught her up easily with his long-legged stride. 'You know he's going to blab, right? Sooner or later?'

'Yup.'

'And what happens then?'

He shrugged. 'She'll come round. She's just a product of our home life. We grew up kind of insecure. She wants to keep him safe from everything.'

He fell in beside her and they walked for a few seconds. 'So, I guess we'll be neighbours as of tomorrow.'

She knew it, yet still the idea was hard to get used to. She glanced at him and he smiled at her and she wished she hadn't. There was an easiness about him that was dangerous. Not evil or sinister, just a threat to her sensibilities. He knew he was sexy. He didn't flaunt it but it was there in every move, every nuance. He had a confidence about him that was breathtaking.

'Oh, goody, skater boy in a suit. It'll be worth it just for that,' she quipped, giving his grunge look a disparaging once-over.

He laughed and she felt like she'd just been dipped in a vat of warm sweet molasses.

'A suit? Me? Hate to disappoint but these are my work clothes.'

Madeline stopped and stared at his fashionably faded long shorts with ragged edging and frayed pockets and his trendy purple striped shirt, unbuttoned and flapping in the breeze. Her eyes lingered at the tantalising glimpse of smooth chest.

She stared at him incredulously. '*This* is what you wear to work?'

'Well, I do usually button my shirt.' He grinned.

She shook her head and started walking again. 'Are you sure you left Melbourne under your own steam? You weren't run out, by any chance?'

He laughed and it felt as though he was licking the molasses from her skin.

'I was a little unconventional for Melbourne,' he admitted. 'Just another reason I moved north.'

Madeline stopped at the light and they waited for it while Connor pushed the button continuously.

The lights changed and they stepped onto the road.

'The other being Connor?' she asked.

He nodded. 'And the weather. It's hard to skate in layers and I love to surf…but I'm getting too old for Victorian sea temperatures. Way too cold.' He shivered, thinking about it. 'Here I can do both all year round. In next to nothing.'

She looked at him again and at his open shirt, trying to block out the images his words were conjuring up in her head. She did not want to go there.

'Well, you've certainly come to the right place,' she managed eventually.

'I couldn't agree more,' he said lightly.

She felt the full force of his gaze and his lazy smile and his dimples and she forgot how to breathe for a moment. 'So, any other reasons for the big move?' she asked, to force herself to breathe again.

He thought about it for a moment. 'My ex,' he admitted.

'It's not amicable between you and your ex, then?' she asked, latching onto a topic that would hopefully wipe his sexy smile off his sexy lips.

'Depends.'

'On what?' she asked.

He shrugged. 'Phase of the moon?'

He was frowning now. That was good. 'Never a dull moment, huh?'

'Oh, it's not too bad, really,' he said. 'A couple of blips along the way. Let's just say moving away was a good thing. For both of us. It was more than time to cut the umbilical cord.' And if he'd only done it earlier, the impulsive event on the eve of his departure might never have happened.

Madeline heard the wistful note to his voice and forgot about the traffic and the other people around them. He sounded vulnerable and she walked on, hyper-aware of Marcus's arm as it occasionally brushed hers, lost for something to say.

'But, hey, I don't want to put you off,' he said after a long pause in the conversation. 'Just because marriage wasn't for me doesn't mean that it won't work out for you and what's-his-name.'

'Simon,' she said automatically, as she put one foot in front of the other.

'Of course, while distance is good for exes, it kind of sucks for couples.'

'Yes, thank you, Marcus. I do believe I've already heard your theory on that. Have you forgotten we live in the same city?'

'Doesn't matter if you live in the same apartment if you never see each other,' he said.

'We're fine. Really.'

The smile she gave him didn't quite reach her eyes but she sure sounded convinced so who was he to question? He'd certainly made a screw-up of his own marriage so what qualifications did he have to judge how other people conducted their relationships? Different strokes for different folks.

He realised as he kept a close eye on Connor that despite only knowing her for three days she'd got to him—more than just physically. He'd seen more of Maddy emotionally than he'd seen of most women he'd known for months, even years.

He'd seen her furious—spitting chips, her eyes glittering angrily at him. Deeply sad when she'd talked about her sister. Sassy when she'd been teasing him about his hocus-pocus. Professional when he'd help her resuscitate Mrs Sanders. And then fragile and vulnerable when he had massaged her feet and neck to ease the grip of her migraine.

He cared about what happened to her. The thought of her wasting away in a relationship with an absentee partner was awful. And although there was a line between them that decent guys just didn't cross, he realised he wanted her for himself. Oh, hell! Just what he needed—to develop an obsession with an engaged woman!

Madeline looked over at him and saw the slight chink in his smile and felt guilty. She was pretending that all was well with her and Simon and, no doubt, rekindling bad memories of his failed marriage. Had she rubbed salt into his wounds? She touched his elbow lightly. 'I'm sure there's someone else out there, Marcus. Just for you.'

'Oh, God! I hope not,' he said as he continued walking.

Madeline heard the vehemence in his voice. Boy, his ex

had sure done a number on his head. 'You shouldn't let one bad experience put you off,' she persisted, catching him up.

'Oh, yes. Yes, I should,' he said.

'But—'

'Maddy,' he cut in, 'it's OK. I like it this way. I date. I have fun. I keep it light. No promises. I wouldn't have it any other way.'

It sounded horrible and she stifled a gasp. At least she knew now what an involvement with him would mean, should she be stupid enough to ever contemplate it. Just because the man had given her a fever that no amount of paracetamol would cure, it didn't mean they were compatible.

'So what? It's just sex? Just flings?' She shook her head in disgust. 'I could never get involved with someone like you. What about commitment? Love?'

'Been there, done that. Paid the lawyers and all I got was a lousy T-shirt.'

She looked at him sharply and saw he was laughing at her. 'I don't think this is very funny.'

Marcus smothered his mirth. 'Sorry.' He held up his hand. 'Look, I have a skewed view. I know that. My mother has three divorces to her name, my hardly-ever-there father two and me one. I have two sisters that are divorced and one who's a single mother. Not good odds. But, hey, I'm sure you and Simon are going to be blissfully happy.'

Why did he make it sound so silly? So quaint? His criticism of Simon came back to her and she was severely ticked by his casual attitude to something that deserved more than that.

She stopped walking, suddenly not wanting his negativity anywhere near her. She veered off to the side of the footpath and held up her hand at a passing taxi.

'What are you doing?' he asked.

'I'm tired of this conversation and I don't want to walk with you any more.' She smiled sweetly. 'So I'm getting a taxi.'

The cab on the opposite side of the road indicated it was turning around for her.

'Very mature,' he said.

She could hear the smile in his voice but refused to look back at his open shirt and his damn six-pack. 'I thought so.'

The cab pulled up and Madeline waved at Connor as she opened the door, throwing over her shoulder, 'Oh, Marcus, talking about mature, I'm sending you a patient called Connie first thing in the morning. Does that suit?'

He eyed her suspiciously and liked how her eyes glittered and her cheeks glowed. 'She's a mess, isn't she?'

She laughed. 'Well, you're the one with the crystal ball— you tell me.' And she slid into the taxi and shut the door.

'Did you make her mad, Uncle Marcus?' asked Connor, coming to a sliding stop beside him.

Marcus winced. 'I think so…'

'She'll never be your girlfriend if you make her mad, Uncle Marcus.'

Great. Dating tips from a six-year-old. He smiled down at Connor and they watched Maddy's taxi disappear from sight.

He knew two things. One, he loved a challenge. And, two, Madeline Harrington, as unavailable as she was, was completely and utterly delicious.

CHAPTER FIVE

MARCUS had half an hour before the arrival of his first-ever patient in his new practice. He could smell the nose-hair stripping aroma of paint, built up to near toxic levels from the offices being shut up all night, and he quickly opened all the windows. He placed an incense stick on the front counter and lit it to help disperse the chemical odour.

He wandered into his office and approved of how it looked. It was tranquil, the neutral wall colour had the slightest hint of green and natural light filled the room from the skylight he'd had installed in the ceiling. On two walls he had a sequential series of framed paintings. The scenes depicted a rainforest at different times of the day. Marcus loved their restful quality.

On the wall where his desk was positioned he had his framed qualifications because, more often than not in his line of work, people demanded to see them. He smiled, thinking about it—no one ever asked their GPs for their qualifications! On the fourth wall there was a variety of different charts. One was a map of the iris for iridology purposes, another the foot for reflexology, and the last one mapped the human chakras.

Many of his conventional medical colleagues who grudgingly accepted his homeopathic beliefs balked at the mention of chakras or zones of energy within the body. As a university-trained medical doctor he knew that such ideas didn't have any foundation in Western medicine. But he also knew that illness was multi-factorial and that everything needed to be taken into account, including the metaphysical.

He sat at his desk in his swivel chair and turned it until he was facing the shut cupboard behind him. He opened the doors and pulled out one of three wide shallow sliding drawers and looked with great pleasure at the rows and rows of little brown remedy bottles. He picked up a couple, ran his finger over the labels, replaced them and shut the doors.

He pushed away from the desk and went into the room next door, which he had set aside as his massage room. He was a fully qualified masseur with certificates in remedial, deep tissue and sports massage, as well as specialising in Bowen therapy.

The massage table was in the centre of the room. An old-fashioned dresser that he had bought at an antique store was at the far end and held all his towels and equipment such as essential oils, CD player and CDs. The walls were the same soothing colour and the ceiling had a rainforest mural painted on it, the central skylight representing the sun and its life-sustaining energy.

He was pleased. It felt much more like his own place than his office in Melbourne ever had. He had inherited that, along with the client list from a retiring colleague, and because it had been part of an office complex with strict limitations on alterations and was already a really successful practice, Marcus hadn't felt able to put too personal a stamp on it.

But here it was all his and the thought made him proud as he walked out to the reception area. It looked like any other doctor's reception with one exception—no secretary. Unless he became exceptionally busy, Marcus planned on doing the reception stuff himself.

Consultations were usually lengthy so it wasn't as if he had to juggle a hundred patients a day. In fact, ten patients a day was his upper limit. And in between clients he could use the state-of-the-art computer system on the desk to update client information and note their progress.

A few fat squishy leather lounges, sourced from op-shops, gave it a retro feel and the wall art was modern but restful. There was a variety of magazines, from alternative health glossies through to the tabloid press. And a large wooden toy box full of things to occupy little hands.

On one of the walls there was a wire rack that boasted a variety of informative pamphlets concerning common illnesses and homeopathic remedies. These were put out by various natural therapy bodies and held lots of good common-sense advice.

Marcus was just switching on his *Sounds of the Rainforest* CD as Connie opened his sliding door.

'Ah, my first customer. Good morning, Mrs Fullbright. These are for you,' he said, presenting her with a bunch of flowers he had bought from the florist on his way in.

'Oh, my,' said Connie, placing her hand against her chest and beaming at Marcus. 'What on earth for?'

'First-ever client in my new practice,' he said, grinning at Connie as she turned a lovely shade of pink. 'These things should be celebrated.'

'Oh, I don't know, Dr Hunt,' she said. 'Perhaps you should wait until after the consultation. See, I'm a bit of a conundrum. I'm afraid I can be a bit of a bother.'

He saw the joy the flowers had given her slowly disappear

from her face. She looked at him with the air of someone eager to be liked but certain she wouldn't be.

'Excellent.' He rubbed his hands together and smiled at her reassuringly. 'I love a good puzzle. This way,' he said, gesturing for her to precede him.

They entered his office and he indicated the chair opposite his for her to sit in. 'May I call you Connie?' he asked. She nodded her head and he continued, 'OK, tell me what's been bothering you, Connie.'

'I'm just so tired all the time. Some mornings it's such an effort to get out of bed. I swear if I didn't have lunches to make and kids to get off to school, I just wouldn't bother getting up at all.'

Marcus nodded sympathetically, his mind already ticking over. 'And how long has this been going on for?' he asked.

'I don't know. Seems like for ever. Dr Harrington seems to think I'm just going through the change…maybe she's right. I don't want to waste your time,' she said.

'Nonsense,' said Marcus. 'In all likelihood it's probably a combination of things. Why don't we start right back at the beginning? Tell me about yourself.'

Connie looked at him, slightly surprised. 'What do you want to know?'

'Everything,' he smiled.

'OK…' she said.

Marcus laughed at her hesitation. Most clients, particularly those who'd been on the rush and hurry merry-go-round of general practice, found his consultations hard to get their heads around. He really had to convince them it was OK to hear their life stories. 'Really, Connie, it's OK. Start at the beginning.'

'What? From the time I first started feeling tired?'

He reached across the desk and covered her hand with his. 'No, from your birth,' he said.

Connie felt tears prick her eyes as Marcus's steady blue gaze assured her it was OK to start at the very beginning. A doctor who wanted to know all about you? They actually existed?

Marcus had to really encourage Connie to start with. She kept stopping. Self-editing. She'd start to say something and then think better of it. He would make a joke or say, 'Hey, Connie, don't hold out on me' and eventually her monologue flowed and she forgot about leaving anything out and unburdened completely.

A client's first consultation could take up to two hours and it was a counselling session more than anything. They were so used to having ten minutes tops with their doctors that being able to vent and unburden was a unique experience. But Marcus wasn't there to just treat symptoms. He treated the whole person. And to do that he needed a very thorough history.

Except for acute cases, his clients and their illnesses were usually the sum of many factors. Add to that the problem of his services too often being sought as a last resort after myriad Western medicine interventions had been tried, and he usually had a very complex puzzle indeed.

The key to unravelling the puzzle was information. As much as he could gather. And remembering that physical symptoms couldn't be treated in isolation. That people's emotional issues were an integral part of the complaint and directly connected to their illnesses.

And that's what he loved about his job. Looking at the person as a whole. Looking at someone like Connie and knowing that somewhere among all the information he was gathering was the key to her treatment.

He made notes as she talked and he could see a really good picture of her as a person in his head. Connie talked about how awful she felt most of the time—depressed and tired. How her joints ached from time to time and she so often felt that there was no hope for her.

Her relationship with her husband was strained. He sounded very demanding of her and wanted everything to be neat and clean and ordered all the time. She spoke about how stressful this was as she could barely drag herself out of bed most days, but she worried he'd be cranky if she didn't so she forced herself to do it. Housework that used to take an hour would take all day as she kept having to stop for a rest.

Marcus was thinking that Connie had classic chronic fatigue syndrome but she'd not spoken about a viral history. 'Have you ever been laid really low by a virus, Connie? Has Dr Harrington ever mentioned glandular or Ross River fever or cytomegaly virus?'

Connie shook her head emphatically. 'No. Never. I've never had a dramatic illness, just lots of little niggling things.'

They talked some more. 'You know the worse part of all this? I took up a floristry course a couple of years ago, through TAFE, you know? I just wanted to do something for me for a change. And I had to quit a month later. I just couldn't concentrate. It hurt to think. It was like my brain was exhausted.'

'Brain exhaustion', Marcus wrote in his notes and ringed it with his black pen. 'Had you been ill around that time with anything?'

She thought for a long moment and then shook her head again. 'No,' she said. 'Only flu.'

'Flu?' Alarm bells ran in Marcus's head. Flu? Influenza? Virus.

'Sure. Actually…it was quite a bad one. Does that count?'

'Most definitely,' he said.

Too often people didn't think of flu as an illness. People just accepted that every few years they'd get it, feel awful for a couple of days and get over it. They often never even thought to mention it to their doctors.

'Yes,' she said, sitting up higher in her chair and leaning forward. 'I was really sick now I come to think of it. Never had flu like it. Lay in bed for three days with huge temps and violent shaking.'

Bingo, thought Marcus. He'd just demonstrated perfectly the need for a thorough consultation.

'You know…I don't think I've been the same since.'

Marcus smiled at her triumphantly and she returned it shyly.

'Do you know what's wrong with me?'

'Yes, I believe I do,' he said.

'Really? Can you fix me?'

'I think everything you've described is classic chronic fatigue syndrome.'

Connie gasped and looked horrified. 'Oh, no. You mean I'm going to be like this for ever?'

'No, absolutely not,' he said, and smiled at her reassuringly. 'I have a very good success rate with CFS.'

'So did flu cause it?'

'We're not sure what causes it but it does seem to be triggered by viruses that leave your immune system weak. I think your case is also complicated by impending menopause, but that's OK. We can treat both.'

'You can?' said Connie.

He squeezed her hand because she looked so hopeful but was trying hard to control it in case he was offering her false hope. 'I can,' he said, and swivelled in his chair to his remedy drawers. 'A dose of influenzinium first then some kali phos,' he said, searching through the alphabetically sorted bottles.

The influenzinium would treat the initial flu complaint and then the kali phos, made from potassium, helped nerves recover, relax and regain power and thus strengthen Connie's immune system. He talked to her about diet and exercise to help with her menopause symptoms as he dispensed the remedy.

Another part he enjoyed about his job. He was the also the pharmacist. Of course, being a qualified medical doctor, he could write scripts as he saw fit and there would always be certain situations where he would prescribe Western drugs. That was the beauty of being both a doctor and a homeopath.

He filled two fifteen-mil empty brown glass bottles almost to the top with a purified alcohol solution. Into one he dropped in a low-potency dose of the pure kali phos remedy. And then mixed the influenzinum into the other. He kept the dosage down as people could have reactions to homeopathic remedies as well, and it wasn't uncommon to experience a worsening of symptoms before noting an improvement.

He screwed on the eyedropper lids and banged the bottles a few times against the table and then the palm of his hand. This was called succussing and was vital to mix the remedy and disperse the energy. Next he added labels to the bottles with the name of the drug, directions for use, the date and Connie's name.

'Take this,' he told her as he passed her the bottle of kali phos. 'I want you to have dose of the influenzinium now,' he said, unscrewing the lid. Connie opened her mouth and he dropped some of the remedy onto her tongue.

'You may have a reappearance of the flu symptoms

again,' he said. 'If that happens, take another dose of the influenzinium but only once. Tomorrow take the kali phos as directed on the bottle. You should start to feel an improvement quite quickly. Ring me if not. And come and see me again next week so we can monitor how you're going. OK?'

'Oh, Dr Hunt,' Connie said as she gripped the little brown bottles for dear life. 'Thank you, thank you. I feel better already just knowing that I'm not going mad.'

He laughed. 'I aim to please.'

Marcus opened the sliding door and waved Connie goodbye. An ambulance was pulled up outside Madeline's practice and she was talking to two paramedics who had an elderly man on their trolley. He strolled over as they were loading the patient.

'Maddy,' he said.

She squinted at him in the harsh morning sunlight and had to remind herself that although he looked dressed for the beach in his hibiscus boardies, he was actually practising medicine. Of sorts, anyway. 'Marcus,' she acknowledged with a tight smile.

'I've just had the pleasure of meeting Connie Fullbright,' he said.

She smiled broadly this time. 'Character, isn't she?'

'CFS,' he said, and watched as her face displayed the usual scepticism shown by a lot of general practitioners.

'So is it to be eye of newt or wing of bat?' she asked sweetly.

He laughed. 'Neither. Just wait and see.'

She stared after him as he walked back to his practice, still chuckling.

* * *

The next afternoon, Madeline was just finishing off some charts for the day and about to head home when there was a knock on her office door.

'Come in,' she said, not bothering to look up from her chart, figuring it would probably be Veronica with some lab results.

'Hello, Madeline.'

Madeline almost drew a line down the page so startled was she by Simon's voice.

'Simon,' she said, pen poised in mid-air, not quite believing he was there. He looked embarrassed and he shuffled his feet nervously. She waited for the joy to come. For the triumph. For the rush of love. Or at least a rush of lust. But it didn't. She didn't feel anything.

'Can we talk?' he asked.

She nodded her head and indicated that he sit in the chair on the other side of the desk. She watched him as he positioned himself and fiddled with his tie. He cleared his throat and Madeline braced herself for what he had to say.

'I made a mistake,' he said. 'I miss you, Madeline. I'd like to try again.'

Madeline felt a whoosh of air leave her lungs. This was the moment. The one she'd been waiting for for two months. Where he would go down on bended knee and ask her back. The reason she still had her ring on. Except now that the moment had arrived she knew with horrible certainty that going back to Simon was not an option.

Sitting here facing him, a mere metre away, she realised she didn't feel anything for him any more. Probably hadn't really for years. He was a nice guy and she liked him, he was a good friend, but where was the zing? There was no leap of her pulse or a delicious squirming feeling down low. She thought back to the massage Marcus had given her and felt like a thousand worms had been released inside her, a really inappropriate surge of heat in her belly. If Marcus had been sitting a metre from her, her system would be in a complete dither.

'Why?' she asked finally.

'I was stupid. I think we'd been together so long that I needed a break to make me realise just what I had. I love you…we love each other.'

No. They didn't. Just hearing the words come out of his mouth brought an immediate rejection to her lips. God, why had it taken her so long to see? 'No, Simon, we don't,' she said gently. 'We've been together for ever. We like each other. We're best friends. We've been through some tough times together. But we're a habit. That's not love. Not love as it should be when you're thinking of entering into a marriage.'

'And yet you're still wearing your ring,' he said, reaching across the desk, taking her hand and rubbing the diamond with his thumb.

'That's because until this moment I really believed we would reconcile. I've been counting on it since you called it off. Waiting for it. But now it's here I realise that I don't want it. You did us a favour, Simon. And I think you know that, too, deep down. I think you walked two months ago because we weren't fulfilling you either.'

She watched him digest her statement. She couldn't believe the words coming from her mouth or that saying them didn't leave her devastated in the least. His dear face and his nice smile were so familiar to her and she'd never imagined it would end like this or that she would feel so disconnected from him. She'd just always assumed that they'd be together for ever.

He's an idiot. She remembered Marcus's words and found herself yet again comparing the two men. Similar looks but complete opposites! Skater boy engendered none of the things that she so admired in her fiancé. *Ex-fiancé.* In fact, her feelings for Simon seemed bland when she compared them to the storm of emotions that Marcus evoked. Simon stirred her loyalty, Marcus stirred her hormones.

Sure, it was purely physical—his smell and his blue eyes and his dimples and his laugh and the way his leg muscles bunched and relaxed as he walked and the fascinating strip of chest hair that disappeared behind his waistband and the way he never seemed dressed—hardly a basis for a relationship. But it couldn't be ignored.

She didn't think Simon had ever worn a shirt unbuttoned in his whole life. She focussed on Simon again, sitting before her, looking genuinely contrite, and knew even a week ago she would have taken him back in a flash. But that had been then. Now Marcus had awoken her sexuality, she was a whole new woman, and she knew she could never just settle for going through the motions again.

'Have you…have you met someone else?'

Madeline started guiltily at his question. 'No,' she denied a little too quickly, and swallowed as images of Marcus massaging her practically naked body sprang into her mind. She hadn't. She refused to feel guilty when she'd done nothing. She thought about her erotic dreams. No, damn it. People were allowed their fantasies.

'I wouldn't blame you if you had,' he said gloomily. 'I can't believe how badly I've stuffed this up. I do still love you, you know.'

'Sure.' Madeline nodded. 'And I you. But we don't love each other the way you're talking about. I love you as a friend. As someone who helped me through some very bad times and knows me probably better than anyone. But that's not enough, Simon. Not any more. And if you were really honest with yourself, you'd know that, too.'

'But maybe if we gave it another try…'

She sighed. 'OK, Simon, answer me this. What did you feel when you first walked through the door? When you saw me again for the first time.'

He thought for a moment. 'I felt home.'

'Exactly,' she said gently. 'After two months apart all you felt was a sense of coming home? You should have felt love and passion and anticipation. You should have heard a symphony in your head. You should have felt like tearing all my clothes off.'

Unbidden, her mind formed an image of Marcus. Now, there was a man whose mere presence made her want to tear fabric.

'And you didn't because we just don't have that type of relationship, Simon.'

'That's just lust, Maddy. That's not important. Not as important as a deep, enduring love.'

'It is important if you don't have it, Simon.' She felt for him. He looked miserable. 'Don't you want it, too? Don't you think you deserve it, Simon? Because you do. You deserve to be with someone who can't keep their hands off you.'

He smiled a weak smile. 'That would be nice.' A few moments passed and then he asked, 'What did you feel when you saw me?'

'Surprise,' she said. 'And then none of the things that I expected to feel. Like, yes, thank God he's back. Or, God, he looks so good he's making my eyes ache and if I don't kiss him right now I'm going to die. I felt…nothing.'

He nodded slowly, then got to his feet. Madeline did, too.

'I'm sorry, Simon.' She shook her head and shrugged. 'Are you going to be OK?'

'Of course,' he said, smiling sadly. 'I know you're right. I guess after a decade together I just…missed you when you weren't around any more. Hardly a good basis for a marriage, I suppose.'

Madeline smiled. 'Look, there's someone out there for you,' she said. 'Someone who's going to make you so happy. I just know it.'

She felt a ball of emotion in her chest take her by surprise. It was really over. Ten years of her life and the reality could no longer be ignored. As much as she knew it was the right thing to do, it was still hard saying goodbye to someone who had been such a huge part of her life.

'I hope we can still be friends,' she said, 'there's too much history to stop being part of each other's lives.'

'Of course.' He smiled. 'I wouldn't want it any other way.'

Madeline smiled back and removed his ring from her finger, holding it out to him.

Simon shook his head. 'Keep it. It's been on your finger for four years. It belongs to you.'

He held out his arms and she curled the ring into her palm and accepted his parting hug. She held him tight, grateful beyond words to have known him for a decade. But it was impossible to be held by him and not compare. His hands on her back were nice, comforting. Marcus's hands made her tremble. Made her hot. Made her needy.

Simon eventually turned and left and she stood staring after him for a long while, the claws of the ring cutting into her palm. To her horror she could feel tears in her eyes. 'I am not going to cry,' she muttered. 'Absolutely not.'

And then promptly burst into tears.

CHAPTER SIX

I SHOULDN'T still be crying, Madeline thought as she determinedly wiped the tears from her face. I've been at it for an hour now—enough. She'd given the official end of their relationship its due, grieved for the closing of a wonderful ten-year friendship, because honestly that was what it had been more than anything, but now it was time to stop.

Madeline stared into the rippling water below. From behind her somewhere the soulful beat of modern jazz drifted to her on the breeze, as did the excited laughter of children splashing around at the nearby city beach. The wake of a passing River Cat disturbed the surface and brought her out of her reverie.

She'd been sitting on the low wall that ran beside the Brisbane River at South Bank for half an hour. The waning rays of sunlight reached across the water, glittered on the surface and caused a kaleidoscope of colours to sparkle in the depths of the diamond ring she still held in her palm.

The tears were gone and she knew that to be fully free so she could move forward, the ring had to be gone, too. She looked at the river and smiled. Veronica would be completely horrified at what she was about to do. The only thing the receptionist had thought any good about Madeline's relationship with Simon was the ring. She'd tell Veronica she sold it, but tossing it into the river had an air of finality she couldn't ignore.

She closed her fist, lifted her arm, drew her hand back behind her head and flung her arm forward. A fist closed around hers from behind, halting the ring-hurling process. Madeline got such a fright she nearly fell off the wall.

'What the—?' she said, as she quickly turned around.

Marcus. Her startled heart settled a little when it realised there was no immediate danger to her life but took up a different tempo, a slower, louder throb, as she recognised that this man posed an even bigger danger than that. He was a danger to her sanity.

A tantalising thought slithered into her brain like the serpent in Eden. *Rebound sex.*

No. Damn you, Veronica.

He was wearing boardies, which were damp, a button-up shirt worn Marcus-style—unbuttoned and flapping open. He had obviously dried himself hastily. His dark chest hair was still damp and she could see a lone water rivulet tracking its way down his washboard abs. His hair was wet and he had a damp towel around his neck. His feet were bare and sandy.

Rebound sex.

No!

He opened her hand, saw the ring and plucked it off her palm. He looked down into her eyes and could see she'd been crying. Something had happened. 'You know it's against the law to litter, right?'

Madeline laughed and turned back to the river view because he was so gorgeous she wanted to bite him. She could feel his presence behind her, feel the heat radiating in waves off his body.

Rebound sex.

Enough already!

'Maybe you should think about this.'

His voice was low, his mouth close to her ear, and she shivered. Part of her wanted to scream at the unfairness of his effect on her, part of her wanted to lean back into him and rub herself against him like an appreciative feline.

Rebound sex.

I mean it, get a grip!

He sat beside her, facing the wide paved walkway, and watched the ebb and flow of human traffic for a few minutes. He was conscious of their arms brushing occasionally and of the weight of the ring in his palm and the hum deep in his loins as his mind wrestled with the possibilities. Did this mean the engagement was off?

'What happened?'

She sighed. 'Simon and I split up.'

Marcus couldn't tell from her voice whether that was a good thing or a bad thing. But she'd obviously been crying so she must be upset. Despite the delicious potential, Marcus had an unexplainable urge to go and find her too-busy ex-fiancé and punch him on the nose. 'Want me to beat him up?' he asked.

She laughed, the humour in his voice making it sexier than ever, and the urge to rub herself against him intensified. She looked at her hands instead, desperately trying to banish the serpent's whisper and not think about rebound sex when they were talking about a serious issue. 'Actually, we split a couple of months ago.'

'Oh?' Marcus said, a little confused. So all this time he'd been lusting after an engaged woman and she hadn't?

'I've been in denial.'

Marcus looked at the bling in his hand and again thought what a fool Simon was to have ever let Maddy get away. He turned side on. 'I told you he was an idiot.'

She smiled. 'No. He did us both a favour. We were together for all the wrong reasons. We didn't love each other. Not like we should have. I just didn't realise it until he came back this afternoon and wanted to reconcile.'

'How did he take it?'

She shrugged. 'Quite well. He knew, too. Deep down, he knew. I'm sure he hasn't spend an hour crying about it like I have.' She laughed.

Marcus nodded. 'So, if it's all over and has been for a while, why the tears?'

She shrugged. 'We've been together for a long time and now it really is over. It feels a bit like he's died, I guess. These things need to be mourned. Trust me, I'm an expert on mourning.'

And tossing the ring was the funeral. He picked up her hand off her lap and placed the ring in her palm. 'Well, I still think he's an idiot,' he said, and grinned down into her serious face, her lips touched by a slight smile. 'Do it. Send the idiot to a watery grave.'

Madeline looked at him through suddenly glassy eyes, warmed by his support even if it was just to cheer her up.

Rebound sex.

She shut her eyes and ignored the whisper as she closed her hand around the flashy piece of jewellery and tossed it long and hard at the pliant river. There was too much noise to hear it plop but she opened her eyes in time for them to both watched it hit the surface and disappear.

'C'mon.' He nudged her arm with his after a few moments. 'I'll buy you a drink.'

She eyed him dubiously, his bare, flat abdomen tantalising in her peripheral vision. 'You're not exactly dressed,' she pointed out.

'This is South Bank.' He shrugged. 'No one cares.'

She did. The way she was feeling at the moment, if he didn't cover that delicious chest she was afraid the temptation would become too great and at some stage she would lean over in mid-sip and run her frosty glass down his perfect abs.

Marcus saw a flare of desire heat her green eyes and the hum in his loins kicked up to a buzz. 'I'll button up,' he said. 'I'll even put on some shoes.' He swung a backpack off his shoulder and brought out a pair of trendy bulky sandals.

'Come on,' he said, and held out his hand to help her around and off the wall.

She took it reluctantly and dropped it immediately she had her feet on the ground. 'Where to?'

'There's a good pub. It's got a great menu. I don't know about you, but I'm starving.'

Madeline faltered and was thankful she was no longer touching him. She was absolutely starving, and he looked totally edible. She suppressed the urge to lick her lips and lean in to gnaw on his neck. 'Famished,' she said.

Marcus heard the husky quality of her voice and noticed the flare again, and began to think that being with Maddy tonight, fresh from her break-up, was maybe not the best idea. There'd been something between them from their first meeting and she was a free agent again. Fair game.

But he knew how she felt about relationships and even if he hadn't, just one look at the delicious Maddy was enough to know that she didn't do casual. And he didn't do permanent. And, besides, coming on to her two hours after her long-term relationship had broken up was just plain icky.

They walked without talking. Fitness freaks jogged around them, power walkers paced past them, families with toddlers and prams dodged them and the sun slowly set around them. They pushed their way through the crowds thronging the night markets and made it to the pub before the beer garden had filled up for the night. They got a table and Marcus left to get them a drink.

The music she had heard earlier was coming from a band inside the pub and the music drifted out, creating a pleasant atmosphere. She could smell beer and peanuts and steaks cooking and felt surprisingly good. The laid-back vibe of the pub was just what the doctor ordered.

'One chardonnay,' said Marcus, placing her drink on a coaster in front of her.

Or was Marcus the remedy? He sat opposite her, gave her a sexy dimpled grin and took a long swallow of his beer. He licked the froth from his lips and she almost groaned out loud.

She felt hot suddenly, hot all over, and she shrugged out of her navy pinstripe jacket and hung it on the back of the chair. When she turned back she noticed he was looking at her. Intently.

'What?' she said, lifting her arms and checking out her crisp white figure-hugging shirt, wondering if she'd spilt something down her front. It was one of those new stretch fabrics and it pulled tautly across her cleavage, the button struggling to keep in place. Maybe a button had popped?

Marcus wondered how much longer the button could stay in the hole and hoped he was around when it finally gave up the battle. 'Nothing,' he said. 'Nice…shirt…' He sounded lame, even to his own ears, and he took another long pull of his beer.

Madeline stilled as she watched his lips press against the

frosty glass. Hang on a minute. Had he just checked her out? She felt as if a finger had stroked across her pelvic-floor muscles as they clenched involuntarily. Maybe she wasn't the only one with a serpent in her head. She leaned back in the chair and noted how his gaze followed the straining button. Interesting. Very interesting.

'So,' he said, placing his beer glass back down and blinking a few times to clear the haze that had descended when he'd thought about what kind of bra she might be wearing underneath. 'Do you want to talk about Simon or get drunk and forget him?'

She laughed. 'That doesn't seem like quite the right thing to do.'

'Do you always do the right thing, Maddy?'

She thought about it and thought about how she so didn't want to do the right thing tonight. How she wanted to throw caution to the wind, down her chardonnay in one mouthful, grab his hand and demand he take her home to his bed.

She swallowed. 'Pretty much.'

He nodded thoughtfully as he kept one eye on that teasing little button. No surprises there. The waitress came and took their order and he was pleased for the distraction. He ordered a T-bone. She ordered pasta.

'OK, so no Simon.'

'No, we can talk about him. I promise I won't burst into tears.'

'Really?' Marcus had three sisters and his mother was on her fourth husband. He'd been privy to more than one bust-up in his life. In his experience women tended to cry for days.

'Sure. You can test me if you like,' she said, and laughed self-deprecatingly. She noticed Marcus's gaze wander back to her chest as her breasts bounced with her laughter. She shifted slightly in the chair and felt her pelvic floor contract again as his gaze followed her movement.

'No tests, I promise. You said you were together a while?'

She nodded. 'Ten years.'

Marcus had to refrain from spitting his mouthful of beer all over her. *A decade!* He swallowed the mouthful and whistled instead. He couldn't even begin to contemplate being with someone that long.

She laughed at the rank incredulity on his face. 'How long were you and your ex together?'

'Three years. Married for two.'

'Yeah, I guess it is a long time.' She shrugged. 'We've actually known each other since kindergarten but got really close after his mother died. My mum had not long gone either so I understood what he was going through.'

Mutual grief? Didn't sound like the best basis for a relationship. Marcus was surprised it had lasted a year. He watched her as she spoke. She was staring into her wineglass, one hand twirling the stem, the other arm bent at the elbow, the fingers absently worrying the knot of hair at the nape of her neck, working it loose strand by strand.

'What happened with your parents?'

'My dad died in a car accident. I was just starting grade twelve. And my mum was diagnosed with breast cancer two months later and lasted nine months. I'm sure her broken heart hastened her end.'

Marcus heard the anguish hidden behind her controlled delivery. His first instinct was to pull her into his arms and comfort her. His second was to run like hell. He took a sip of his beer, acknowledged the dangerous zone he was entering and took a mental step backwards. He was buying her a drink and a meal and seeing her home, and that was it.

But then she sighed loudly and gave up on the strands, pulling the pins out instead, throwing them on the table as she raked her hands through her hair until the knot loosened and the curls sprang gently around her shoulders. He watched, fascinated, as her body moved, as her neck twisted from side to side, as her breasts jiggled with each arm and shoulder movement. And the button maintained its precarious hold.

Dear God. He couldn't run now if he wanted to. He had a sudden vision of that hair spread on his pillow, wrapped around his hand, trailing across his body, and tried to remember why hitting on a woman who had just ended a relationship was a bad idea.

'Sorry, this must be depressing the hell out of you,' she said, shooting him a sad smile as she picked up her wineglass and sipped the dry white appreciatively.

He laughed. 'And this from the woman who sent me Connie Fullbright.'

They laughed together and Marcus pointed to her nearly empty wineglass. 'Another?'

Madeline hesitated. For a second.

Rebound sex.

'Sure why not?' The wine was giving her a pleasant buzz that, combined with Marcus's obvious appreciation, was quite exciting. She deliberately adjusted her collar and noted Marcus pause as he rose, his eyes widening as his gaze followed the path of her fingers as they lingered near the holding-it-all-together button at her cleavage.

He continued on his way to buy another round but not before Madeline had seen the bob of his Adam's apple and the flash of desire glitter in his eyes. She smiled to herself. So this was sexual power? How could she get to her thirties and not know how heady it was?

Rebound sex.
God damn it. All right, all right!

Marcus approached her warily from behind, praying that he had himself together now. There was something different about her tonight that trebled her sexiness. Even from behind she stood out from the crowd. Her gorgeous crop of lush red ringlets falling to her shoulders separated her from every other woman in the pub.

'Thanks,' she said, as he put her wine down.

He smiled and they both tasted their drinks. She crossed her legs and brushed her foot against his bare calf. 'Oh, sorry,' she said, smiling at him over the rim of her glass.

Marcus almost choked on his beer. The contact had been too slow to be accidental. It had lingered a little too long. He gave her a searching look and she held his gaze steadily. He'd seen that look before. Great! He was going to be rebound sex? Not that he had anything against it *per se*. Hell, he'd been used on more than one occasion on the rebound and had enjoyed himself immensely.

But he remembered not that long ago he had stupidly been rebound guy for his ex and it hadn't been his wisest moment. Maddy was emotional and he didn't want her to confuse his intent. He would probably see her most days—it would be smart to keep things between them strictly business.

'Tell me more about Abby,' he said, grabbing the first thing that popped in his head and then wished he hadn't. 'Sorry, no, bad choice. I'm supposed to be cheering you up.' He just needed to get her off track. Because if she came on to him, he thought, trying not to stare at that damn button, he wasn't sure how good his powers of resistance would be.

'It's OK, I don't mind talking about her.'

'You blame yourself for her death?'

She sucked in a quick breath. How had he had seen so deeply inside her on such short acquaintance? 'Of course,' she said in a small voice, and shrugged. 'I was her older sister. I was supposed to be looking after her. Just before my mother died she said to me, "Look after Abby, she's impulsive, she'll need you." For God's sake, I was practically a doctor. I should have been able to save her.'

'What happened?' he asked gently.

'She'd been gone for a few days. We shared a flat close to campus, she often stayed over at her boyfriend's unit. I wasn't concerned.'

'What was she studying?'

'She was doing an aromatherapy course,' Madeline said. 'She was always a bit alternative. You would have loved her.'

He laughed and took a swallow of his beer waiting for her to continue. She was leaning forward on the table again, her elbow bent, her palm cradling her chin. He could see the creamy rise of her cleavage.

'Then late one night Nathan, her boyfriend, came to my door, with Abby in his arms. He was really upset. She was sick, he said, and strode past me, laying her on the lounge.'

Madeline stopped for a moment and took a sip of her wine. She could still see her sister's face and feel the horror when she had realised Abby had been desperately ill.

'She was burning up, barely rousable. Nathan told me they'd taken her to a psychic surgeon earlier in the day and he'd removed her appendix and given her some white powder for the pain. She'd been asleep most of the day but had woken feverish and doubled over. The autopsy showed her appendix had ruptured and she'd had raging peritonitis.'

'Nasty,' Marcus said quietly.

She nodded. 'I was furious but there was no time to rant and rave at them. Call an ambulance, I said. I tried to rouse her but couldn't. And I couldn't do anything. I didn't have any oxygen or a doctor's bag or anything. I had nothing to help her. Nothing. All I could do was wait and pray that the ambulance would make it in time.'

Her despair felt as raw today as it had five years ago. 'Did they?'

'Nope. She arrested a few minutes later. But just prior to that her eyes flicked open. She was trying to say something and I had to get right up close to her mouth to hear it. She said, "Don't be mad, Maddy, you've been the best sister."'

Madeline stopped and swallowed, trying to control the emotion that had risen in her chest. 'I think she knew she was dying.'

Marcus saw a tear track down her face and she dashed it away. He leaned closer with both his elbows on the table and covered her hand with his. 'Did she die in the flat?'

She shook her head, not trusting herself to speak. She took a deep breath before answering. 'Officially, no. She died *en route* to hospital but she'd been in full arrest for five minutes before the ambulance got there and they spent another half-hour working on her. I don't know how many times they shocked her but I wouldn't let them give up. She's septic, I kept saying like a demented idiot, "She needs fill. Fill her up, fill her up."'

She stopped again, surprised as ever how raw the pain still was sometimes. Marcus's hand on hers was comforting and the one thing that was keeping her anchored in the present. Without it she would have been sucked totally into the past and that terrible day.

Marcus sat quietly, stroking his thumb across her

knuckles, letting her remember, her story incredibly moving. 'You said there was an autopsy?'

She nodded and cleared her throat. 'Her organs had already started to shut down. She was in DIC.'

'So…there wasn't anything you could have done that would have changed the outcome? Even if you'd had every medical knick-knack and machine that went ping?'

She smiled and slowly withdrew her hand. 'No. And I know that, rationally. But in my heart, deep in my gut…she was my sister. My little sister, you know? It's wrong that I couldn't do a thing.'

Her eyes pleaded with him to understand and he did. When love was involved, right and wrong blurred and blame always came into play.

'And then I get angry with her sometimes and I feel guilty about that, too. I mean, why on earth would she go to a psychic surgeon? That's taking alternative a bit too far, right? And Nathan said she'd insisted that he bring her to me instead of the hospital. Wouldn't let him call an ambulance. Why? How stupid was that?'

Fairly stupid. Nathan had been as well. He chose his words carefully. 'She did make some unwise choices,' he agreed.

'It was just so unnecessary,' she said. 'Such a waste of a life.'

He nodded. 'Yes, it was.'

'It was awful. I was in my final year of med school. Simon was amazing. So supportive. I don't think I could have got through that time without him. He's the only one who knows how bad it was. It bonded us.'

'I'm pleased he was there for you,' Marcus said, and meant it. Maddy had had a lot of tragedy in her life. It just didn't seem right that one person had had to shoulder so much. He was pleased that Simon had served a purpose, even if it meant they'd developed an unhealthy codependency.

'Sorry I came on so strong at you in the beginning. I guess now you know why. It just makes me so angry sometimes.'

'Understandable,' he dismissed quickly. 'What happened to the…er…psychic guy?'

'Nothing. A slap on the wrists. He didn't actually operate on her, just made her think he had, so he couldn't be charged with her death.'

That made Marcus angry. Alternative medicine struggled so hard to be recognised because people like that quack constantly destroyed their credibility.

Their meals arrived then and they were both pleased to have their conversation interrupted. They ate for a while, savouring the food, Madeline grateful to take a break from talking about herself. 'So now you know all my deep dark secrets. What about you?'

He chuckled as he cut into his steak. 'Nothing too deep and dark about me, I'm afraid.'

'Hah! Don't believe you. What about your ex? What happened there?'

'Ah.' He smiled. 'Long story.'

She smiled at him as she slowly sucked a strand of fettuccine into her mouth and watched his eyes bulge ever so slightly as her tongue darted out to lick some creamy sauce off her lips. 'I'm not going anywhere,' she said.

He stared at her for a moment, trying to clear the lust from his brain. 'We were twenty-two,' he said after a moment. 'She got pregnant, we got married. She had a miscarriage. The whole thing was a disaster. We got divorced.'

She laughed. 'So that's the nutshell version?'

He shrugged. 'It was a long time ago.'

She rolled her eyes. 'Men! I just tell you all my gut-wrenching stuff and you give me nutshell? I want more,' she demanded with a smile.

'All right,' he sighed, resigned to a full dissection of a time in his life he'd rather not remember in too much detail. 'What do you want to know?'

She looked at him exasperatedly. 'I don't know…' She searched around for something to start with. 'What's her name?'

'Tabitha.'

'How long were you together before she got pregnant?'

'A year.'

'Did you love her?'

'I think so, in the beginning. But I think I was more besotted with her than anything. She was the prettiest girl I'd ever seen. It wore off kind of quickly, though. I was about to call it off when she discovered she was pregnant.'

'Ouch!'

He laughed. 'Indeed.'

'But you married her anyway?'

He nodded vigorously. 'No way in the world was a kid of mine growing up without a father. Been there, done that. Wouldn't wish it on my worst enemy. I insisted we get married.'

Madeline nodded. That made sense, knowing what she knew about his childhood and his bond with Connor. 'How long after that did she miscarry?'

'About a month. She was sixteen weeks.'

Madeline whistled. 'Late. She must have been devastated.'

He nodded. It had been so unexpected. Tabitha had been well into the second trimester—it had been a shock.

'And how did you feel?'

'Truthfully?'

She nodded.

'Relieved. Sure, it was sad, too, but I wasn't ready for a baby. As much as I ranted about my child having a father, I lived with this constant feeling of dread. Like my life as I knew it was at an end. I mean, we were so young and we'd tied ourselves down to marriage and children and I was in med school and trying to study and work to support us. And then I felt guilty that I was relieved and stayed for another two years, trying to assuage my guilt.'

She gave him a sad smile and reached her hand across the table and laid it on top of his. 'Poor you.'

He smiled back. 'Poor Tabitha. I think I stayed in Melbourne for so long because I still felt that guilt years later. I've tried to be there for her since. You know, do some DIY stuff, helped her move house a few times, checked in on her from time to time.'

'She's not remarried?'

'No. She's had a few relationships that haven't worked out.'

'And neither have you,' she said speculatively as she withdrew her hand.

He laughed. 'I'm a fast learner.'

A waitress came and removed their plates and took orders for another drink. They moved onto other topics and Madeline found herself relaxing. The music was good, the company was very good and her third glass of wine was amazingly good.

With their angsty conversation behind them, the thing between them flared again and Madeline enjoyed her newfound power. Her every move, every gesture was followed intently by Marcus's interested gaze. She pushed the envelope purposefully. Her fingers caressed the fine chain at her neck, fiddled with her wristwatch and her arms folded and unfolded, drawing his gaze repeatedly to her cleavage.

Marcus was charming and easy to talk to and when he laughed it lit up his whole face and emphasised his dimples, and the noise was rich and deep and soothing. As the night settled around them and the flames from the garden torches danced shadows across his jaw stubble, the feelings he had stirred with his massage intensified. The longer she spent in his company, the surer she was that Marcus was just what the doctor ordered. *Rebound sex.*

'Dessert?' he asked.

Only if she could be it. She looked him straight in the eye and shook her head. *Rebound sex.*

'Coffee?'

She held his gaze steadily and shook her head again. *Rebound sex.*

Marcus felt his groin tighten. He looked at his watch. Nine p.m. 'Then I guess we should probably go.' They were at one of the last remaining occupied tables, most people having left as soon as they'd eaten.

She nodded and stood. She draped her jacket over her arm and retrieved her purse, giving him a twenty-dollar note.

'I think I can manage it,' he said.

She considered him for a minute. He looked like he could manage it very well indeed. *Rebound sex.*

She shrugged. 'OK. Thanks.'

They walked past the markets, now closed for the night, and back towards the river. They ambled down the walkway in silence, the fairy-lights in the trees that lined the far side providing a subdued glow. They didn't talk for a while.

Madeline could feel her heart pounding in her chest as she

debated ways to proposition him. It had seemed like a good idea in the pub but thinking it and doing it were two different things. She could hear the gentle lap of the river and the warm evening air was filled with the fragrance of summer blooms.

But his arm brushed hers occasionally and she could smell his aftershave and the faint whiff of beer, and when he walked slightly ahead of her his gait was all man and his butt was as cute as hell.

'Actually, I wouldn't mind a coffee,' she said. 'Why don't we go up to your place?' Her heartbeat thundered in her ears and she held her breath.

Marcus stopped. His loins felt on fire. He knew what she was suggesting. He turned back. 'There's plenty of coffee-shops still open,' he said, holding her gaze.

'I haven't seen your place yct,' she said.

Marcus sighed. 'Maddy…'

Madeline almost groaned out loud at the way he said her name. Her muscles clenched. 'Please, Marcus,' she said quietly.

He walked over to the wall where she'd been sitting earlier and looked at the darkened river, shimmering in places with the reflections of the city lights. He turned back and wished he hadn't because she'd obviously been standing just behind him and was now, consequently, just in front of him. And then she took a step closer. He placed a staying hand on her shoulder.

'Maddy…' he groaned.

'Please,' she whispered.

He shook his head and took a side step away from her. 'No,' he said. 'You need to stop this.'

'Are you going to make me beg?' She smiled despite his rejection because he looked so conflicted. Poor guy.

Marcus shut his eyes to block out the images her begging evoked. 'Look, you're on the rebound.'

Madeline's smile widened. Yeah, hence the rebound sex! 'You don't want to be rebound guy?'

Of course he wanted to be rebound guy. But he didn't really think she knew the rules. 'You said yourself that you could never be with someone like me. You're a commitment girl. I respect that. Rebound sex.' He shook his head. 'There are rules, Maddy. It's not about love or relationships. It's just about lust and desire and sometimes even there's a healthy dose of revenge thrown in.'

'Good,' she said, stepping closer again. She didn't care about the happily ever after stuff for tonight. She got it. Tonight was just about sex. 'So now I know the rules.'

'If we do this—'

'When,' she interrupted with a smile and reached forward to trace his collar-bone with her finger.

He felt the jolt in his groin and grabbed her hand, holding it still. 'If,' he said pointedly. 'You need to know that it's probably not going to mean the same thing to me as it is to you. It'll be sex—'

'Good sex?' she interrupted again.

Hell, yes! She looked set to ignite at the merest touch. 'Concentrate, Maddy. I don't do weddings or babies or long term. You've just heard why. From a female point of view, my commitment track record sucks quite frankly,' he said, trying to lighten the mood.

'OK, OK,' she said, moving in so the length of her body was now touching the length of his. 'Just sex. I get it.'

She didn't care and she certainly didn't want to get involved with someone else on the back of her split with Simon. Especially a commitment-phobe. But Marcus's hard body felt so good she was going to scream if she didn't feel him in her as soon as possible.

'Are you sure, Maddy? Really sure?' he asked, his voice husky, her lips millimetres from his.

She stepped back and smiled at him. 'Cross my heart,' she said, doing the actions in a flirty lingering fashion, feeling the arousal of her nipples. 'Your place or mine?'

'Mine,' he said, grabbing her hand hastily and pulling her along. 'It's closer.'

They didn't talk, just walked. Quickly. By the time they reached the foyer of his apartment complex they were both breathing harder. They waited impatiently for the lift to arrive and the second Marcus had punched the number six and the doors had pinged shut he backed her against the wall and gave her a hard probing kiss. Madeline almost fainted as the tightly controlled lid she'd been keeping on her hormones exploded and she kissed him back like he was a freshwater stream and she was dying of thirst.

She dropped her bag and her jacket to the floor and hooked a leg around his. She felt Marcus grip her bottom and he pulled her up and in, grinding his pelvis into hers so she could feel his desire. She whimpered and a surge of moisture dampened the junction of her thighs.

The lift pinged and he dropped her back onto her feet hastily. He squatted down in front of her, looking up into her emerald eyes, his nostrils flaring at her female scent. He hastily picked her things up off the floor, grabbed her hand again and half strode, half ran with her down the hallway to his door.

Madeline stood looking at the door as he fished through his pocket for the keys. She noticed the number on his door was sixty-nine and she quirked an eyebrow at him.

'That a promise?' she asked cheekily, running her fingers over the brass numbers.

'Absolutely.' He grinned, his belly suffusing with heat. 'Whatever you want.'

'Hurry,' she said, her voice low, husky with desire.

He laughed to hide the slight tremble of his fingers as he fumbled to unlock the door. His hand shook, his vision blinded in a cloud of lust. He relaxed as the key finally slipped into the lock and he opened the door, pulling her inside, slamming the door behind them and pushing her back against it.

And then he was kissing her and his hands were everywhere. He wanted to take her here, now, against the door, but he wanted to taste every part of her first.

He pulled back and she mewed her disappointment. He chuckled and gave her another hard kiss on the mouth. 'It's OK, I just want to look at you.'

Madeline watched as his gaze fell to her cleavage and his index finger stroked lightly against the little white button that had winked at him and teased him all night.

'This,' he said, 'has to go.' And he grasped the lapels of her shirt and yanked the shirt open, buttons popping and flying everywhere.

Madeline gasped and laughed, not caring that he'd just ruined her shirt. The look of pure male need as he gazed at her breasts hardened her nipples as quickly as if he'd applied ice cubes.

'Oh, my God. Green and pink lacy push-up,' he said, staring at the twin marvels like they were chunks of precious stone. 'With a little jewel in the middle. Front clasp.'

He looked at her and gave her a slow sexy smile. 'Pictured you as a white-cotton girl,' he murmured.

His dimples winked at her. 'Never judge a book by its cover,' she said, wishing he'd kiss her again. He ran his fingers down the lacy edge of the bra, delving into her cleavage, stroking and teasing the soft skin.

'Matching knickers?' he asked, leaning in to kiss the slope of her neck and reaching behind to the zip of her skirt, sliding it down and easing it off her hips.

She kicked out of it and blushed as his appreciative gaze devoured her body. Her matching knickers met with his approval and she thanked God nice underwear was her one true vice.

'I'm going to lick you all over,' he promised her, then swept her up into his arms. He kicked open his bedroom door and within three strides had dropped her on his bed.

He took a moment to just look at her. Her Titian ringlets lay fanned out on his bed. Her green and pink lacy underwear hid and emphasised all at once.

'Marcus,' she whispered, and held her arms out to him.

'Tell me what you want, Maddy.'

Make love to me. It was on the tip of her tongue but she stopped herself at the last moment. She didn't want Marcus to think she was unclear about the rules. 'I want you in me now.'

She watched as his dimples disappeared and his clear blue eyes hazed over with lust. 'Good answer,' he said as he tore off his clothes.

Madeline admired his nudity, the broadness of his chest, the definition of his muscles and the length and hardness of his erection. Her fingers itched to touch and she licked her lips in anticipation. And when he lowered his body onto hers she revelled in the weight and the feel and the hard jut of him cradled against her pelvis.

He kissed her and she almost cried it was so good. As his tongue stroked across her lips and delved into her mouth she reached down between them and stroked the smooth hard length of him. His deep moan was empowering and she boldly positioned him at her entrance.

'Now, Marcus, please. Now.'

He tore his mouth away. 'Oh, no. I said I was going to lick you all over and that's exactly what I intend to do.'

'I can't wait that long,' she panted.

He chuckled. 'I'll make it worth your while,' he teased.

She shook her head. 'I mean it, Marcus. It's been too long. I need to feel you in me or I'm going to go insane.'

She wriggled her pelvis so his head was teasing her entrance and she clutched his back convulsively as she felt herself flower at the stimulus. 'Please, Marcus. Please.'

'But—'

She lifted her head and kissed him hard on the mouth. 'No buts. You don't need to worry, I'm more than ready for this.'

He grinned. 'At least let me get you naked,' he teased.

'Nope.' She smiled back. 'Right here, right now. Like this.'

He reached for a condom and tore the packet with his teeth. 'What the lady wants…' He shrugged.

Madeline braced herself for his entry. His hands fumbled her knickers aside and as he slowly pushed inside her he pulled aside one lacy bra cup. She opened her eyes in time to see his downcast head as his mouth feasted on an erect nipple.

She bit down on her lip to stop the scream as his full length pulsed inside her. 'More,' she moaned, and almost fainted as he pulled out and plunged back in again, harder, faster this time.

She whimpered and she could feel his body tremble against hers. 'More,' she said, louder this time.

Marcus had never been this turned on in his life. Maddy's nipple was a hard peak in his mouth, scrapping erotically against his tongue, and her hot moist depths milked him as he plunged to the hilt.

'Faster,' she groaned.

His mouth left her nipple and plundered her soft lips, silencing her demands. They were making him build too quickly and he wanted to stay there for ever.

'Oh, Marcus,' she said, tearing her mouth from under his. 'Don't stop. Don't you dare stop!'

'No chance, Maddy.' He laughed, burying his face in her neck and licking his way back down to her still hard nipple.

Madeline felt on fire. His first plunge had lit the fuse and with each thrust the flame moved slowly towards flash point. He was on her and around her and in her and she could feel him and see him and smell him and she wanted him to pound inside her for ever, hold her like this for ever.

But she could feel the first twinge of her orgasm and knew it was going to end soon. She needed it, desperately, but fought the pull, still reluctant to end their union.

She groaned out loud and Marcus rained kisses on her face. Another groan was ripped from her and she gave herself up to the sensations, not caring that she would most likely be dragged under and drown in the undertow. She'd go happily.

'Marcus,' she panted. 'There. Oh, God, don't stop. Marcus!'

He picked up the tempo, thrusting harder, faster as his own orgasm rushed up from deep in his loins. He groaned her name, too, as he felt her contracting around him, giving him the extra stimulus, sucking him under as well.

They cried out together as their bodies shook with the intensity and they rode it until the pleasure became so severe it was painful and neither could go on any longer.

Madeline's breath was ragged as the remnants of pleasure undulated deep inside her, stroking him, still hard inside her. She revelled in his weight and the unevenness of his breathing and knew he was as incapable of movement as she was.

As she lay in the aftermath, his weight pressing her into the bed, she knew that she'd never previously experienced what she'd just experienced. Never in a decade with Simon. Never. Ever. And it wasn't just the sex. Somewhere, while she had been drowning in the undertow, she'd made a much more intimate connection.

The ice that had encased her heart was gone. Melted like a snowball in sunshine by the heat and intensity of Marcus's passion. In a few days and one cataclysmic night he had thawed what she hadn't thought could ever be thawed. Her heart pulsed in the warm cavity of her chest again and she had him to thank for it.

Rebound sex.

Oh yes!

CHAPTER SEVEN

Now that she had tasted the sweet addictive fruit of great sex, Madeline was insatiable. She was an addict. Her body craved it. All night. And Marcus didn't disappoint. Not even once.

Madeline had never had such athletic sex in all her life. But, hey, she thought as she snuggled into his shoulder, listening to his deep even breathing as the first rays of dawn crept across the sky, at least she now knew she was capable of a marathon.

But it had been more than that, it had been fun. She'd had fun. Marcus had been flirty and humorous. He had made her laugh, he had made her blush and, God help her, he had made her come more times in one night than she had ever thought possible.

She'd never known she was capable of such an amazing feat. Sure, she'd experienced orgasms before but they'd always been hard won. Marcus had barely even touched her and she had combusted every time. How he did it she didn't know, she didn't care, she just never wanted him to stop.

She couldn't believe she had been fooling herself for an entire decade. She *was* a sexual being and she wanted to yell it from the rooftops. And she wanted more. As much as he could give her. She had a lot of catching up to do. She yawned and smiled as sleep finally claimed her.

Marcus woke a couple of hours later, the weight of Madeline's head on his chest. He looked down and her red ringlets were spread across his chest just as he had fantasised about when they had first met. Their marathon sex session in all its glorious detail came back to him and he smiled to himself.

He hoped she wasn't through using him for rebound sex yet. OK, rebound sex rules were very clear—it was a one-off deal. But it wasn't like these rules were written anywhere and as long as they were both still on the same page, then what could it hurt?

He picked one of her curls up and stretched it out gently. The sun slanting through the blinds caught a golden high-light, transforming it to a strand of fine gilt thread. He dropped it and stroked his hand over her head and down the length of her hair, feeling the springiness beneath his palm.

She murmured and he stopped, not wanting to wake her. If she was half as tired, half as exhausted as him, she was going to need to sleep for a week to get over it. He smiled again, thinking about her generosity in bed, and there was a strange tightening in his chest.

He shifted slowly, gently displacing her, preferring not to dwell on that odd sensation. He was also experiencing a tightening elsewhere and knew it was time to get up or he and Maddy would never make it to work today. He sat on the edge of the bed and looked behind him, running his eyes up and down the length of her body. She'd rolled on her back, her legs tangled in the sheets, her stomach and breasts uncovered.

The urge to trace a finger between her breasts and down

her stomach beyond the sheet was overwhelming and he stood immediately. He strode into the *en suite* and turned the cold water on hard, catching his breath as he stood under the cold stinging needles.

Madeline vaguely heard the running water and slowly opened her eyes. She stretched and then curled into a ball as her internal muscles protested. The bed was empty but she could still smell Marcus's aftershave and she hugged her body and smiled to herself as she remembered every Technicolor detail.

She got up and wandered into the *en suite*. Marcus stood with his arms braced against the wall, facing the shower head, his head down, his eyes shut, the water running down his back.

'Good morning,' she said as she opened the glass shower door and stepped inside. 'Enough room for two?'

He opened his eyes and smiled at her. She was beautiful and he wanted her again. 'Of course,' he said, moving back.

She smiled at him and stepped under the spray, gasping and flinching at the unexpected temperature, her body facing his. She shut her eyes and ducked her head under the water, allowing it to run all over her naked body. She could feel Marcus's eyes on her and again felt the thrill of sexual power.

Marcus swallowed hard as he watched the water run over her breasts, the cold scrunching her nipples instantly, down her flat stomach and cling to the red curls at the juncture of her thighs. She opened her eyes and caught him staring and he didn't care. She gave him a flirty, knowing smile and he shook his head at her. 'Tease.' He grinned.

'This water is freezing,' she said.

'I know. I needed it,' he said, reaching past her to add some hot.

She grinned, her heart thudding loudly, her excitement building. 'You didn't wake me,' she chided.

'No,' he said, electricity thrumming through his veins, 'but I wanted to.'

'Well, for that, I'm going to have to punish you,' she said, her voice a light flirty teasing.

He chuckled. 'Oh? What did you have in mind?'

Madeline smiled at him, turned on by the mere thought of what she was about to do. She pushed him back against the shower wall and stood as far away as his erection allowed. She looked at him, holding his gaze for as long as she could bear it, and then knelt before him.

Marcus shut his eyes and groaned loudly as her warm lips and hot mouth closed over him. If this was a punishment, he was going to be bad for ever.

'Oh…my…God,' he groaned, and gave himself up to the pleasure.

Madeline made it to work just in time for her first appointment. Marcus had dropped her home so she could change her clothes and she had waved him goodbye reluctantly.

She plonked her briefcase on her desk and sat in her chair, absently swinging herself round and round. She felt exhilarated despite her two hours' sleep. She couldn't remember having felt this alive in a long time. She felt like she'd been in limbo for so long, starting with her parents' death and perpetuated by her guilt and grief over Abby. She'd stayed in an insane holding pattern with Simon for so long, and when he'd said goodbye two months ago, it had been one more person who had left her.

Today she felt like she was actually moving forward with her life. And she had Marcus to thank for that. And she would, she thought smiling to herself as she called her first patient in, the very first chance that came her way.

Mrs Wust, her last patient before lunch, sat at the desk and Madeline was pleased she'd soon be able to take a break. Her concentration had been completely shot and more than one patient had commented on how tired she looked.

'Jet lag?' Mrs Wust enquired after the usual pleasantries.

'Er, yes, must be,' Madeline said. An image of Marcus living up to his apartment number came to mind and she felt heat suffuse her cheeks. 'Now, did you have that ultrasound?'

The patient handed the films over to Madeline and she put them up on the viewing box, easily identifying a gall bladder full of stones before reading the report.

'Well, it is as I suspected, Gail. Your epigastric pain is due to gallstones. I'm afraid you're going to need an operation. I'll give you a referral to a surgeon and he can discuss your surgical options,' said Madeline, opening her drawer and re-trieving her stationery.

Gail Wust's face fell. 'Oh, no. Isn't there another way?' she asked.

'Well, it's done laparoscopically these days so the scarring and recovery time are minimised. It's really only an overnight procedure nowadays.'

'No, I mean naturally. A friend of mine was telling me that her brother's wife's sister-in-law used an old-fashioned oil and lemon juice recipe to cure hers.'

Madeline looked at Gail, her pen poised. She was the typical cholecystitis patient—fair, overweight and in her forties. Not that long ago Madeline wouldn't have even en-tertained a natural remedy but a lot had changed in a week.

She tore off the page she had been writing. 'I'll refer you

to Dr Hunt. He's a GP who specialises in natural therapies who's just moved in next door. I'm sure he'll be able to guide you.'

She was surprised at how calm her voice sounded, given how much her hands were trembling as she wrote her neat, precise referral. She put it in an envelope and passed it over to her patient.

Gail reached for it and Madeline pulled it back just in time, a plan forming in her mind. A plan that was making her squirm in her seat just thinking about it. 'Actually, Gail, I might just drop it next door for you now and discuss your case with Dr Hunt. I'll get him to give you a ring to arrange an appointment in his next available slot. OK?'

After Gail had gone, Madeline rose and visited the bathroom, quickly pulling off her knickers and stuffing them into her handbag along with the written referral.

'I'll just be next door for lunch,' she said to Veronica with as much serenity as she could muster, given she was naked under her skirt.

'OK,' said a surprised Veronica, looking up from her work. Since when had Madeline done anything other than have a quick sandwich and a cuppa at her desk?

Madeline blushed as people in the waiting room nodded and smiled—did they know she wasn't wearing any knickers, or were they just being polite and acknowledging her? She felt completely naked, the glide of the skirt lining over her bare bottom bordering on erotic.

She was grateful to escape the office—Veronica had a nose for gossip and she looked well and truly on the scent. She walked out into the sunshine and inhaled madly. This was crazy! What was she doing? This really wasn't something she ever did and she wondered if she had the gumption to carry it out. But she remembered his kisses from the previous night and knew she couldn't live another minute without feeling his lips on hers again.

As she slid back his door she had a moment of panic that last night had been a one-off. She felt out of her depth, unsure of the etiquette. She faltered.

'Come on through. I'm in my office.'

Marcus's sexy voice was the clincher and she walked towards it like a moth drawn to flame. She reached his doorway and leaned on the jamb, appreciating the view. He glanced up and smiled a sexy dimpled smile and a hand clenched her insides.

'Well, hello,' he said, sitting back in his chair and admiring the view himself. He saw she'd tied her hair back and remembered how it had been spread across his chest that morning when he'd woken up, and he itched to pull it out.

'Hi.' She smiled back, drinking him in.

Neither of them spoke or moved for a while, images of last night's nocturnal activities rendering them incapable of anything other than breathing. And even that was strained as each remembered the intimate details.

Marcus recovered first, smiling at their stupor. 'To what do I owe the pleasure?' he asked, and then grinned at the way her body almost swayed at his choice of phrase.

'I brought you this,' she said huskily, walking closer to his desk on shaky legs and tossed the referral onto his desk.

He picked it up, inspected it for a second and glanced back up at her. 'Is that it?'

His voice was hoarse and she could feel her nipples peak at the gravely quality and the anticipation. 'No,' she said, delving through her bag. 'These as well,' she continued, taking a deep breath and lobbing her red knickers onto his desk.

The jolt in his groin was instantaneous. He looked at them. Then at her. Then held them up, unscrunching them so he could appreciate their prettiness. They were soft and silky with lace in the right places and two little bows each side holding the back and front together.

'Are these spares you keep for emergencies?' He grinned at her.

She grinned back. 'No, I took them off five minutes ago,' she said, and it was her turn to watch his pupils dilate with desire and hear his sharp intake of breath.

She walked back to the door, shut it, locked it and then ambled over to his side of the desk, dumped her bag on the floor, pushed his chair back from the desk and quickly straddled him. Marcus grabbed her buttocks and pulled her down so she could feel his arousal.

'Maddy,' he said, sucking in a swift breath as his erection surged against the confines of his zippered pants.

She grinned at him. 'So, I've been thinking about these rebound rules,' she said, reaching down and slowly undoing the button of his shorts as she rubbed herself against the coarse fabric, almost fainting as it rasped against her naked flesh. 'Are they flexible? Or is rebound sex just a one-night deal?'

Marcus swallowed hard as she felt her hands on his zip and her fingernails deliberately caress him through the fabric. He sucked in another breath and bit his bottom lip, not quite believing he was about to have sex in his office chair with a client only fifteen minutes away.

He gave a half-laugh, running his hands up her bare thighs, under her skirt until he was squeezing her naked buttocks. His vision went completely black at the feel of her cold taut flesh and the urge to drive up into her was all he could think about. 'Extensions can be granted,' he said.

'Good,' she whispered, grasping his finally freed erection in her hand and swallowing his groan as she unleashed a kiss that had half a day's worth of pent-up sexual fantasy behind it. By the time he pulled away they were both breathing hard.

Marcus didn't speak, he wasn't capable. He didn't even take her jacket or shirt off, just pulled her shirt out of her waistband, dispensed with the buttons, more gently than he had last night, briefly admired her matching bra before undoing the front clasp and bending quickly to suck a puckered nipple deeply into the warm wet cavern of his mouth.

Her moan urged him on and he teased the other breast with his hand working the nipple to a tortured peak, all the time excruciatingly aware of the magic her hands were weaving.

'Condom,' she gasped.

He pulled away, breathing hard, admiring the view of her straddling him, her bare breasts heaving and moist from his mouth. She looked gorgeous and wild, her green eyes bright with passion. He reached blindly into his desk drawer, not wanting to miss a second of the view, felt around and produced one.

'Thank God for reps,' he said.

She took it, ripped it open with her teeth and covered the broad length of him in one swift movement.

'You're very good at that,' he said.

'Only that?' she asked as she positioned herself over him and very slowly claimed his length.

'No,' he said, reaching behind her and pulling her hair out of its clasp as he entered her. She shook her head and looked wild and free and then he was inside her completely, throbbing with need. 'You have many talents.'

She smiled and kissed him again and his hands resumed

their homage to her breasts. He thrust up into her and she rode each penetration, revelling in his hardness and the success of her seduction. Each drive stoked her to fever pitch.

She could feel the slow build-up down low and deep, the angle of his entry stroking her in just the right spot, and she moved with it, perfectly in tune to its rhythm. And then it picked up a notch and then another and then more until an explosion of sensations ricocheted inside her, bucking through her. She was conscious only of the tremble of Marcus's shoulders as he joined her, the urgency of his cries mixing with hers.

And then as she collapsed against his chest the intensity eased, pleasure resonating in every cell and oozing from every pore. Languor spread through her muscles, her breath calmed and her pulse settled as her climax slowly ebbed away.

Marcus waited until he got his breath back. 'Many talents,' he said.

Madeline laughed and reluctantly pushed herself away from the curve of his neck. She looked down at herself, half-undressed, her nipples still hard, still intimately joined with Marcus. She didn't feel awkward or ashamed. She looked at him and she could tell he liked what he saw.

A distant voice interrupted them. 'Er, excuse me, Doc, are you here? Is there anyone home?'

Madeline almost injured herself she leapt up that quickly. 'Who's that?' she whispered.

'My twelve-thirty,' he said, amused by the red staining her cheeks and her hurried rearranging of her clothes.

'You have a twelve-thirty? Why didn't you say something?' she hissed. She couldn't believe how close they'd come to being sprung by a patient. Thank God she'd locked the door.

'And miss out on more rebound sex? In a chair? Are you crazy?' He winked, watching with great interest as Maddy jiggled around, trying to pull her clothes into some order. 'I'll be right out, Ted,' he yelled.

Madeline blushed even further. When had she become so bold? She picked up her bag and hurried to the door, unlocking and opening it. 'Right,' she said to Marcus in an over-bright, businesslike voice, 'So you'll follow up on that referral, then?'

He grinned at her. 'Yes, ma'am, Dr Harrington,' he teased. 'Oh, Maddy,' he murmured as she disappeared.

'What?' she whispered, poking her head back around his door.

'I think you forgot these,' he said, throwing back her knickers that had lain discarded on his desk.

Madeline caught them with one hand and blushed again.

'Tonight?' he asked.

Wild horses couldn't have kept her away. 'Tonight,' she said as she stuffed them in her handbag and hurried away, Marcus's sexy laughter following her down the hallway.

Four hours later Marcus showed Gail Wust into his office.

'Thank you for seeing me on such short notice, Dr Hunt,' she said.

'It's Marcus,' he reminded her for the second time, 'and it was no problem. You're lucky it's my first week and it'll take a little while for people to know I'm here.'

'Did Dr Harrington talk to you about my case? I believe she wrote you a referral?'

Marcus didn't blink as he remembered their 'talk'. 'Yes,' he said. 'We spoke.' Kind of.

'She's such a great doctor. A really sweet young woman,' Gail chatted. 'So polite.'

Marcus blinked this time, thinking about how far off sweet and polite she'd been in his office four hours ago. 'Yes,' he said noncomittally, 'very…sweet. So, you have gallstones?'

Gail took the bait and Marcus was relieved to get off the topic of Maddy. It was bad enough that he could still smell her perfume in the air and her scent on his clothes and had been in a state of semi-arousal all afternoon.

He made an effort to concentrate on his patient as she talked about her symptoms of indigestion and then an episode of acute abdominal pain. She gave him the ultrasound images and he popped them up on his viewing box, examining them closely, and then read the report.

'I've heard there is a natural way to dissolve gallstones. Do you know anything about that?'

He smiled at her reassuringly. 'Yes, I've had a lot of success with it in my practice. But I warn you, it's not easy or very palatable and it'll be a good couple of weeks before you can try it. You may be better off having a quick laparoscopic day procedure if you're experiencing frequent attacks of cholecystitis.'

'As long as I don't eat anything too fatty, it's usually OK. Why will I have to wait that long?' she asked.

'We need to make some dietary adjustments first to detoxify your system and prepare the gall bladder properly to pass the stones.'

'Like what?'

Marcus took a detailed history of Gail's dietary habits, formulating her detox plan.

'Well, you've eliminated most fatty foods so that's good, but you'll need to also eliminate the hidden fats like those naturally occurring in dairy foods. You need to halve your protein intake and substantially increase your fruit and veg consumption. And it's very important to increase your water intake to between two to three litres a day so you can flush out the toxins.'

They talked extensively about meal planning and strategies to cope with the detox phase.

'So I'm going to have to do this for ever?' she asked gloomily.

He chuckled. 'No, this is just for the two weeks prior to the elimination procedure. But it is probably a good idea to look at what dietary habits you can modify so the stones don't re-form. It's not about denying yourself, Gail. Just about moderation.'

He wrote on a piece of paper and tore it off and gave it to her. 'Go to the health-food shop and get yourself some lecithin granules. Add them to your meals—it helps to emulsify the cholesterol and reduce the size of the stones. This is really important as bigger stones can damage the neck of the gall bladder.'

'OK.' She nodded. 'So, after the two weeks, what happens then?'

'You can start the procedure. I usually recommend that you do it before going to bed and hopefully you'll sleep through the worst of it. Take a dose of Epsom salts a few hours before that to ensure that once the contents of the gall bladder are emptied into the intestine, they are eliminated quickly. Mix three-quarters of a cup of safflower oil with half a cup of fresh lemon juice—'

'Hmm, yummy,' she said, wrinkling her nose.

'Yes, it's not very palatable but it is effective. As soon as you've taken it, lie on your right side with your knees bent. This is the most anatomically correct position to ensure the oil and lemon juice penetrate the gall bladder. And then, fingers crossed, the bile duct will dilate to expel the oil and the stones will go with it. You should pass the stones in your next bowel motion. Sometimes a repeat procedure is needed if all the stones don't clear first time.'

'Will it hurt?'

'There may be abdominal discomfort and nausea. It shouldn't be unbearably painful. If it is, ring me. But I'll get you to come back in a week and we can talk about how you're going. What do you think?'

'Sounds better than an operation.' She smiled. 'I'm willing to give it a try.'

He smiled and stood. 'Good, we'll make an appointment for next week. Any troubles in the meantime, don't hesitate to ring.'

Marcus whistled a happy tune as he waltzed back into his office. Another satisfied customer. He was confident that Gail would be able to pass her gallstones naturally and pleased that he could make a real difference in people's lives.

And then he walked into his office and Maddy's perfume hit him again and Gail became completely insignificant. He hardened again, thinking about what Maddy had done to him in this very room and, better still, what would happen that night.

The old sensible Marcus warned him against getting too into her and their incredible chemistry. But the new Marcus, the one who had looked down at his chest that morning and seen it covered in her red curls, wanted to throw caution to the wind and follow wherever this thing led.

Maddy Harrington was making him lose perspective. When he was around her it was easy to forget about the commitment-phobe Hunt genes—his divorce-prone parents, his three sisters who had made complete screw-ups of their partnerships and his own failed attempt.

Madeline Harrington blinded him to it all. She was dangerous and he couldn't even muster the energy to care.

CHAPTER EIGHT

THE next six weeks flew by and they were the most incredible of Madeline's life. She and Marcus were pretty much inseparable. He would call in and pick her up from work each evening and they would rush to her place, the closest, falling on each other the second they were alone, like lovers who hadn't seen each other for a century instead of only eight hours.

He was perfect. Life was perfect. It had gone from being in the doldrums and her vigilantly guarding herself from life and love and hurt to being spectacularly wonderful. He didn't put a foot wrong. He was funny and sexy and kind and patient. He was a good cook, a great masseur and a fantastic listener. A true gentleman who opened her door and picked up the cheque. And, in bed, he was adventurous and generous and he just couldn't get enough of her.

And she couldn't get enough of him. Hated being apart from him. Resented each minute without him. And when he kissed her again after a day's absence it was like that first night all over again. Sweet and desperate, lustful and greedy. She'd never known she'd been capable of such passion until now. Or that she could throw all caution to the wind and allow herself to live in the moment for a change.

She'd never done that either and it was liberating. She stead-
fastly avoided thinking about where she and Marcus were
headed, preferring to think only in terms of what they were
doing today.

Because, whether they admitted it or not, they'd moved
far from the realms of rebound sex. In fact, they had broken
every rebound sex rule that apparently existed. Whether they
admitted it or not, they were in a relationship. And she was
damned if she wasn't going to enjoy the perks while it lasted.

Everyone had been surprised. Veronica had been ecstatic.
She kept grinning stupidly at Madeline and muttering stuff
like, "You go, girl," and "Hubba hubba," as she passed by.
Yep, Marcus being in her life had been an absolute sensation.

She knew she had totally blown their minds by her completely out-of-character behaviour. Had she been that boring?
That predictable? She could see, looking back, that she had
been stuck in a rut. Some kind of emotional limbo, studying
hard, living for her work, trying to bury the pain of Abby and
her parents and fool herself that she was in love with Simon.
It was only now that she was living that she truly realised how
disconnected she'd been from real life.

Mary adored him. 'I knew he'd be right for you. About time
you found yourself a young man who couldn't keep his hands
off you,' she had declared to a pink-faced Madeline a few
hours after she had sprung them kissing in her office. Not that
long ago Madeline would have been mortified by her behaviour but now she revelled in it, enjoying the carefree flush
of being desired.

Marcus ushered in his first patient of the day. His practice
had been building nicely. He was three-quarters booked most

days. And his nights were just as full. Maddy was amazing. Life was pretty damn good at the moment.

Jenny Smith entered the room, carrying her six-year-old son, Trent. She sat on the chair opposite.

'Hi,' said Marcus, noting the boy's pallor instantly.

'Ouch,' said Jenny, indicating the specimen jar on his desk, full of gallstones.

Marcus laughed. 'Yes, indeed,' he said holding up Gail Wust's successfully passed stones. 'Thirty of the blighters. Better out than in.'

He remembered how excited she had been when she had come to see him and had given him the stones as a memento. A further ultrasound had showed no evidence of any remaining gallstones and she had been one very happy customer.

So too had Connie who, after two weeks, had had more energy than she'd known what to do with. He remembered how emotional she'd been when she'd thanked him and every couple of days she'd pop in with some home-made cake or biccies to show her appreciation.

'Enough,' he'd groaned at her good-naturedly when she had brought him some mouth-watering Anzac biscuits the other day. 'I'll be as fat as a house,' he laughed.

'Oh, I don't know.' She winked. 'I hear you're getting plenty of exercise these days.'

It seemed as if everyone knew about him and Maddy. The fact that he didn't seem to care should have rung rather large alarm bells. Were they heading into a relationship? Would that be so bad?

'Are you OK, Dr Hunt?' asked Jenny.

Marcus pulled himself out of his reverie. 'Sorry, I was miles away.' He pushed thoughts of Maddy aside. 'What can I do for you today?'

'It's Trent,' she said. 'I think he may need some more vitamins. He's been very lethargic the last few days. We've just moved and I've been putting it down to that and him being off his food again. The naturopath in our old place had him on a vitamin cocktail because he's always been a fussy eater, appetite of a sparrow, and I worry about his nutrition.'

'He is a bit of a skinny Minnie,' said Marcus. 'Pale, too.'

She shrugged. 'He's always been pale.'

Marcus rose from his chair and came around to squat in front of Jenny and Trent.

'Hey, little mate,' he said quietly.

Trent looked at him solemnly and tucked his face shyly into his mother's breast.

Marcus didn't have a good feeling about Trent. Close up he looked paler still. He looked beyond the 'pale-child' label. He looked anaemic. 'I'll just have a little look at him,' he said to Jenny, and indicated that she should lay him on the couch.

Trent lay docilely as Marcus examined him. It was hard to believe that he and Connor were the same age. The boy didn't feel feverish at all but Marcus noted the pallor of his inner lower eyelids and the mucous membranes of his mouth. He felt some enlarged lymph nodes in his neck and lifted the boy's shirt to listen to his chest.

That was when he noticed the bruising. And his bad feeling intensified. He had multiple small bruises over his stomach. 'Has he had these for long?' he asked.

Jenny gasped. 'I noticed a couple when I was dressing him this morning. But he didn't have this many. And he has a couple on his arms and legs, but he's six. He's always falling over and hurting himself,' she said.

Marcus pushed up Trent's sleeves and noted the bruises on his arms and then inspected his legs. He felt in Trent's armpits and groin and found further lumps. A six-year-old with lethargy, pallor, bruising and enlarged lymph nodes. He shut his eyes briefly and hoped to God that he was wrong.

He pulled Trent's shirt back down and indicated that Jenny could bring him back to the desk.

'I want you to take Trent and have these blood tests done right away,' he said to Jenny, writing out a pathology form. 'The nearest place is two blocks away.' He circled the box on the form that said 'Urgent' several times. 'I'll ring them and let them know you're coming and to put a rush on it.'

Jenny took the slip from him. She looked confused. 'What's wrong?'

Marcus chose his words carefully, not wanting to worry her too much at this stage and certainly not when she had to get in her car and drive. 'I think he's anaemic. I want to know why.'

'So…' she said, looking confused. 'Can't vitamins help with anaemia?'

Marcus's heart went out to her. If Trent had what he thought he had, he was going to need much more than vitamins. 'Let's just get the blood results first and then we'll talk about how to treat it,' he said gently.

Marcus saw fear flit through Jenny's eyes as it started to dawn on her that there might be something seriously wrong with her son.

'There's something you're not telling me,' she said. 'I need to know what you're thinking.'

Marcus wavered for a moment. This was always the difficult part. To share his suspicions before they were confirmed to prepare her a little or to keep mum until he knew for sure and completely knock the wind out of her.

'There are lots of things that can cause anaemia,' he prevaricated.

'Yes, but what do *you* think it is?' she insisted.

He looked at her worried eyes and the way she was clutching her now sleeping son to her chest and knew that people always preferred you to be honest with them. He sighed. 'I'm concerned that Trent may have leukaemia,' he said, ploughing on through her shocked gasp. 'But I can't be sure until the results are back.'

'Leukaemia? But he'll die,' she said frantically.

Marcus felt panic roll off her in a tangible wave. Who could blame her? How would he feel if someone was telling him that Connor had leukaemia? Fun-loving, skateboard-riding, daredevil Connor?

'Please, don't let's get ahead of ourselves here. Let's get the tests done and go from there. If he has it then we'll admit him straight to hospital and he can begin his treatment immediately. There is a very good cure rate, Jenny.'

She nodded. 'Will he need chemotherapy?' she asked.

'That is the treatment,' he said.

'What about natural therapies? I've heard enough stories about chemo to know that it's not very nice.'

'No. It can have some awful side-effects,' Marcus agreed, 'but it's the only course of action I would recommend.' Marcus knew that there were complementary methods employed by some alternative medicine practitioners to treat cancers, but the medical doctor in him never took any chances with cancer.

'Oh, God,' she said, her voice cracking. 'I can't believe this is happening.'

Marcus smiled sympathetically, a sudden horrible vision of Connor limp and pale keeping it real for him. 'As I said, let's just take this one step at a time. OK? Blood tests first. Then in two hours I want you to go next door, to Dr Madeline

Harrington. I'm going to get the lab to phone the results through to her. I'm referring Trent's case to her.'

'But I want you,' she said.

Marcus could see Jenny was trying really hard to hold it together. 'I'll be there, too, I promise, but as I specialise in natural therapies I think it's more appropriate for you to have a traditional GP to take over Trent's case.'

Jenny stood, barely disturbing Trent. 'Right. OK. Right. I'll go, then. OK.'

Marcus led her out gently. She looked totally frozen, like she was registering nothing in her brain other than the words 'child-hood leukaemia' in big tall letters. He helped her buckle Trent into his booster seat and handed her the car keys. 'Drive carefully,' he told her, and waited until she looked at him and nodded.

Marcus sat back down at his desk. He wished he felt more positive about Trent Smith's chances. But he'd seen this presentation a little too often to doubt himself.

He dialled Maddy's number. She was with a patient and excused herself for a moment.

'Well, hello,' she said softly, recognising the caller ID.

Marcus felt his lips lift up into a slight smile as her voice curled into his ear. 'Hello to you, too,' he said softly.

Ordinarily he'd ask her something outrageous like what she was wearing and laugh when she acted all prim and proper in front of a client. But today, despite the delicious lurch of his stomach when he'd heard her voice, he just wasn't in the mood.

'To what do I owe the pleasure?'

He could hear the smile in her voice and pictured her holding the phone, her lips against the receiver.

'Business, I'm afraid. Can you clear a space in your

schedule for two hours' time? I have a six-year-old boy that I suspect has leukaemia. His mother is getting his blood tested now.'

Madeline squeezed her eyes shut briefly, her heart going out to the anonymous little boy. 'Are you OK?' she asked, knowing that imparting news such as this also took it out of a practitioner. Knowing how close he was to his six-year-old nephew, cases like these could be a little too close for comfort.

Her low voice tinged with empathy was soothing. On days like this he wished he hadn't come to work. He could have been in bed with her, her low voice whispering scandalous things in his ear instead.

He sighed. 'Yep. Can you swing it?'

Madeline looked at her appointments. She'd swing it somehow. 'Sure. You coming, too?'

'Yep.'

'All right. I have a patient. I'd better go. I'll see you then.'

Two hours later Marcus walked into the surgery, past a grinning Veronica and straight into Madeline's office and directly into her open arms. She felt good. It felt good to be there.

'What are the results?' he asked, pulling back reluctantly.

'White cells astronomical. Critically low platelets and red cells.'

'ALL,' he said despondently.

She nodded. 'Fill me in,' she said.

Marcus went over Trent's case for a few minutes. Then the intercom buzzed. 'Jenny and Trent Smith are here,' Veronica announced.

'I'll bring them through,' he said.

Marcus made the introductions and sat himself on the edge of Madeline's desk. 'I'm sorry, Jenny. The blood tests have confirmed it. Trent has ALL—acute lymphoblastic leukaemia.'

There was silence as they watched the confirmation slowly sink into Jenny's head. She looked at them with tears in her eyes. 'What is that, exactly?' she asked.

'ALL is a cancer of the bone marrow,' Madeline said, stepping in. 'Something goes wrong, we don't know what, that causes an overproduction of immature white blood cells. These crowd the bone marrow, preventing it from making normal cells, like red cells, which is why he's so pale, and platelets, which is why he has bruises everywhere.'

Jenny hugged a listless Trent to her and rocked him, a tear tracking down her face. 'So, what happens now?'

'We want you to go home, pack a bag and take Trent straight up to the children's hospital. I'll ring ahead and let them know you're coming,' she said. 'You'll be seen by an oncologist and treatment will commence immediately.'

'Chemotherapy?' Jenny asked.

Madeline nodded. Poor little Trent, he was going to be put through hell in the next few months, trying to force his body into remission.

Jenny shook her head. 'This is all happening too fast,' she cried.

'Have you told Trent's father?' Marcus asked.

'We've been separated since just after he was born,' she said. 'He doesn't have anything to do with him.'

Marcus shut his eyes briefly. Oh, no. Poor Trent. He remembered how much it sucked not having a dad around and felt overwhelmingly protective of this sick little boy. Poor Jenny. She was going to have to shoulder a huge burden.

'Do you have someone in Brisbane to support you?' asked

Madeline, stepping in for Marcus. She could feel his distress and knew that he wouldn't be able to walk away from this fatherless boy either.

'My mother,' said Jenny absently. 'She's away for five days in the back of beyond, visiting my grandmother. I've tried a couple of times to ring but they're not in and mobile coverage is pretty patchy out that way.'

'Give me the numbers. I'll keep trying for you,' said Marcus. 'Just get Trent to the hospital. That's the most important thing. I'll call in later.'

Jenny's hand shook as she wrote on the pad Madeline provided. She stood, hugging Trent to her for dear life, and Madeline swallowed a lump. Jenny was like so many mothers she had seen in the past in the same situation. Shocked and worried but holding it all together so their child wouldn't get upset. Madeline knew that the minute Jenny had a spare moment alone or her mother walked through the door, she was going to completely lose it.

When Jenny had left they both stared after her, lost in their own thoughts. Days like this were all part and parcel of their jobs but giving horrible news was never a pleasant task. There were many highs in this line of work but the lows really took the shine out of a day.

She moved closer to where Marcus was sitting on the edge of her desk and hugged him around the shoulders from behind. He laid his head back into her shoulder and Madeline kissed his forehead.

'Want to go out and eat somewhere tonight?' he turned to her and asked after a while.

She smiled at him. It would be the first time in six weeks they'd actually eaten first. She understood. 'Sure, sounds good. South Bank?'

He nodded and gave her a slow, sad smile, pushing up off the desk. 'I'll see you after work.'

She nodded and watched him leave the room. The situation with Jenny and Trent had obviously left him as dispirited as it had her.

'Did you get hold of Jenny's mum?' Madeline asked as they strolled to South Bank, holding hands.

'Yes, not long ago. She's flying back to Brisbane early tomorrow morning. I called in and saw Jenny, too.'

'How's she holding up?'

'Barely,' he said. 'They're hoping to start his first round of chemo in the morning.'

'Poor kid,' she murmured, and Marcus squeezed her hand. When she looked at him she knew he was feeling even more wretched.

They walked the rest of the way in silence and without any consultation they ended up at the pub where it had all started only a few weeks ago. They sat at the same table and he ordered them the same drinks and they whiled away the evening eating and talking, trying to keep their minds off the plight of another fatherless six-year-old boy.

But when they ended up back at his apartment, it wasn't the same as the first time. Their joining wasn't the fast, furious, get-your-clothes-off exercise it had been last time. It wasn't flirty or funny. It was one hundred per cent more intimate than any time before. Madeline felt as if her soul had been stripped bare and Marcus had given her a rare insight into his.

Her orgasm was more intense than it had ever been and afterwards he held her to him, not moving away. His weight grew heavy and eventually she stirred and he reluctantly shifted. But he pulled her in tight, her back against his chest, spoon fashion, and he dusted her shoulders and neck and back with feather-light kisses as she fell asleep.

Madeline woke a couple of hours later, Marcus's arm still around her, his breathing deep and steady. She shifted his arm gently, needing to use the bathroom. He stirred a little then rolled on his stomach and drifted back to sleep.

She took care of business then stood in the *en suite* doorway for a few moments, just watching him. Ordinarily she would have gone back to bed and woken him for more sex but his face was free of the frown he'd been wearing all day and she decided to leave him alone.

Feeling restless, she pulled on her knickers and her shirt, fastening one button at the front, and wandered into the kitchen. She put the percolator on and fixed herself a cup of coffee and took it onto the deck, sitting in a chair and putting her feet up on the railing. It was a beautiful night. A three-quarter moon hung large in the sky and bathed the river below in its milky glow.

A soft breeze blew, lifting her heavy curls off her neck, and she shut her eyes, enjoying the kiss of the wind on her heated skin and the sounds of the river below and the background hum of the city all around her. Her thoughts drifted to Marcus's love-making and her stomach flopped over, thinking about how he had made her cry out for mercy from the power of her orgasm.

Six weeks down the track she still couldn't believe how he made her body come alive. He knew every inch of her skin and where to stroke it and where to kiss it and where to lick it. He knew the bits of her that made her shiver, the bits that made her moan and the bits that made her beg for more. She had never been 'known' so thoroughly.

And she knew his special places, too. She knew that if she stroked the sensitive flesh where his hip bone sloped down into his abdomen he would tense and if she licked his collarbone he would break out in goose-bumps, and if she bit his neck he would groan out loud.

She sipped at the coffee, relishing the wave of lust that undulated through her body. If she kept thinking like this she was going to have to go back in and wake him, whether she wanted to or not. She could feel her pelvic-floor muscles ripple in anticipation and she sighed deeply.

She let her thoughts drift to other things and invariably they went to Trent Smith. She thought of Jenny out there somewhere, probably lying awake in the dark, worrying or crying herself to sleep. The fragility and uncertainty of life seemed magnified tenfold by the Smith family's tragedy.

It just didn't seem fair that a little boy, innocent and carefree, was looking down the barrel of a potential death sentence. Yes, these days there was over a seventy per cent five-year survival rate for childhood leukaemia, but you could never be sure who was going to be in the seventy and who was going to be in the thirty.

She realised that you never knew what was around the corner. Trent Smith had been a happy little boy a week ago, a little pale and a picky eater, but essentially normal. And now he was in hospital about to start chemotherapy. If it could happen to him, it could happen to any of them.

It had happened to her parents. And Abby. Happy and alive and in love one day and then three days later on her couch, minutes away from dying. Life was short and unpredictable. She knew that from Abby and now from Trent and she certainly knew it from her line of work.

She thought about how Marcus's heart had melted today

when he'd discovered that Trent's father wasn't around. She knew him well enough to know that it had really affected him. He had a big squishy soft spot inside for kids just like Trent. Kids like Connor. Like the kid he'd once been. She had seen how great he was with his nephew and knew that Trent facing leukaemia without a dad was like pushing a big old bruise inside him that had never quite healed. She loved him for that.

And there it was. She loved him. She hadn't meant it to be. She hadn't planned it. Hell, she hadn't even realised it until this very moment. But the truth was inescapable. She was in love with him. He had warned her not to, he had been very clear that it was just sex, but it had happened anyway.

Quite what the hell she was going to do with her revelation she didn't have a clue. Neither of them had talked about their future. They'd both just been living in the moment. Maybe after all this time his feelings had changed, too? But if they hadn't? What would he do if she told him and he walked? Could she handle it if he did? And was tonight really the best night to spring it on him?

Was there ever going to be a good time? When would have been the right time to tell Jenny Smith about her son? What the hell were her and Marcus doing? Having nights of endless sex and spending every spare moment together was all well and good. But what if she was diagnosed with cancer tomorrow? What if he was hit by a car, riding that ridiculous skateboard? Would she regret not having told him? Did Jenny regret not having told Trent she loved him one more time each day for the last six years?

The mere thought made her sit up straighter and she felt a pain in her heart just thinking about it. She loved Marcus. And she wanted to tell him because her heart was so full of emotion at the moment she wanted to share the magic with him.

But she wasn't brave enough to lose him over it either. She may not have ever intended to fall in love with him but now she was here, she needed to be careful of her heart. He had an ex-wife who had left him with baggage—permanent commitment scared the hell out of him. She needed to tread gently.

Tonight might not be the night for declarations of undying love but she needed something to cling to. Maybe she just needed to start talking about the future a little more? Her feelings a little more. Maybe she could get an acknowledgement that they were more than rebound sex, that they'd moved on from there. That they were in some kind of relationship.

She heard Marcus rustling around in the kitchen a few minutes later and felt her heart pick up its tempo. Strike while the iron was hot?

Marcus stepped on to the deck. 'Here you are,' he murmured, leaning over and kissing her on the head. He could see straight down her top from his vantage point behind her and liked what he saw very much. He put his coffee on the table and nibbled down her neck, his hands sliding from her shoulders down under the collar of her shirt, until he was cupping her naked breast. He rubbed his thumbs over her nipples and felt himself twitch.

Madeline shut her eyes and gave herself up to the erotic rub of his fingers. Her internal muscles tightened and she wanted to stretch and purr like a contented cat.

He growled into her neck and slowly unhanded her. He stood up, collected his coffee and sat in the chair beside her.

They sat in silence for a few moments, looking at the river. He watched the breeze lift her curls off her neck and felt the urge to nibble there return again. 'Penny for them,' he said.

She looked at him, her heart beating a mad tattoo in her chest. Strike while the iron was hot. 'We're not having rebound sex any more, are we?'

Marcus looked assessingly at her earnest face. No, they weren't. It had been an easy thing to continue to believe they were. There had been no insistence from her, no suggestion that it was anything else. No hints they make it more permanent, buy a ring, move in together. But deep in his heart he knew they'd moved into a relationship.

'No,' he said.

She smiled. That was the first hurdle.

He cocked his head and then sipped at his coffee. 'What brought this on?'

'I've been thinking about Trent and Abby and how fragile life can be,' she said quietly.

Marcus nodded. It was hard not to reassess the course of your own life when confronted with someone else's mortality. Especially a six-year-old boy's.

'I think I'm falling for you.' Madeline didn't know where the words had come from and cursed herself for letting them out. This wasn't in her plan. At least her disobedient brain had the good sense to not completely blow her cover.

Marcus blinked. He waited for the alarm bells to start ringing and the denial to spring to his lips. But there was nothing. Just the intriguing possibility that Maddy was actually serious.

'Aren't you going to say something?' she asked a few minutes later.

Marcus stood and leaned against the railing, facing her. He moved her legs, supporting them against his body instead and massaged a foot.

'You know that's not the idea of a rebound relationship

right? You're supposed to just use me for sex. And then have several other sexually based relationships until you fall for someone. I'm rebound guy. You're supposed to use me up and leave me. It's not wise to fall for rebound guy.'

Hmm. So he hadn't rejected her outright. She felt amazingly heartened. 'Sorry.' She shrugged and then smiled, obviously not that sorry at all.

He smiled back. 'Think about it, Maddy. You've been with one person for ten years. You should have a period where you date other men, sample what's out there before you chose from the menu.'

His foot massage was sexy as hell and she was finding it difficult to concentrate on the conversation. She'd found her entrée, main and dessert in one. 'Is that what you want?' she asked. 'You want me to go off and date other men?'

Marcus stopped rubbing her foot. Was it? Hell, no! The thought of another man touching her, being with her, made him want to break things. Made him want to lock her away. She was his, he did things to her, and she did things to him that he'd never experienced before. He had no idea why he was playing devil's advocate. 'No,' he said. 'No, I don't.'

She smiled. 'Good,' she said. 'That's enough for now.'

She dropped her legs down to the ground and walked into his arms. He opened his mouth to talk to her and she silenced him with a deep lingering kiss. 'Don't say anything, just take me inside and make love to me,' she said softly.

Marcus swung her up wordlessly and strode into the lounge, and was making his way to the bedroom when there was a knock at the door. They both stopped and looked at each other, puzzled. It was eleven o'clock at night.

'You expecting anyone?' he asked.

Hardly. It was his place after all. She giggled. 'No.'

He sighed and turned around, carrying her to the door.

She laughed some more and wiggled her legs. 'Put me down.'

'No way, he said. 'I'm not ever letting you go.'

Madeline forgot her embarrassment and clung to him, buoyed by his statement.

'Open the door,' he told her. 'My hands are full.'

She giggled again and opened the door for him. It swung open and Madeline saw a pretty blonde woman standing there, a suitcase at her feet.

'Who the hell is she?' the woman asked Marcus, glaring at Madeline.

Marcus dropped Madeline on her feet quickly, keeping his arm around her waist, not able to believe his eyes.

Madeline didn't know who the woman was but she saw the possessive gleam in her eyes and wanted to roar, 'Back off,' in her most demonic voice. 'Who the hell are you?' she demanded in return, not caring that her shirt barely covered the tops of her thighs and the button holding the two sides together didn't cover very much either.

'I'm Marcus's wife,' the woman said haughtily.

'Ex-wife,' said Marcus firmly, finding his voice.

So, this was Tabitha? She was a pretty little thing. Killer body. Madeline felt ill.

'What do you want, Tab?' he asked, not quite able to believe that she had followed him all the way to Queensland and had chosen this particular moment to announce herself.

'I'm pregnant,' she said, placing her hand protectively on her flat stomach. 'It's yours.'

CHAPTER NINE

'THIS mobile is switched off or not in a service area.'

Marcus left another message and pushed the end button on his phone in frustration. He lay on the couch, staring at the darkened ceiling. Damn Tabitha, damn her. A baby? His baby? *Jesus!* He felt an awful sense of *déjà vu* and quelled his rising panic.

The scene played over and over in his head. Tabitha dropping her bombshell. Him standing there completely speechless. Maddy looking at him for clarity. For denial. And when he continued to look like a stunned mullet, gathering her stuff and leaving with dignity and grace. And him realising in that moment, as she'd walked out of his door, the awful truth.

He loved Madeline Harrington. Had it only been hours ago that she had told him she was falling for him? It seemed like a year. And it seemed like he had gone one better. He wasn't just falling, he had fallen—all the way. Hard. Why had it taken Tabitha walking into his apartment and Maddy walking out of it to finally get it? He loved her. In seven weeks he had gone from being hopelessly intrigued to helplessly in love.

Sure, he had loved Tabitha, about a million years ago now in a weird kind of fashion. But what he felt for Maddy bore no resemblance to his long-ago feelings for his ex-wife. He wasn't a kid playing at grown-ups, as he had with Tab. He *was* a grown-up, with a grown-up love so deep and so enormous it had caught him unawares. He couldn't think how his life was going to be without Madeline. He just couldn't contemplate it.

Yes, things were really complicated right now with Tab and the baby, but he had to make it work, he just had to. There had to be a way to be a father to the baby and keep Maddy as well. It had taken him till he was thirty-five to finally fall in love and he wasn't going to lose it now.

He unlocked his phone keypad again and decided to send her a text. He tapped out the words *I love you* and then hesitated and deleted them. Why would she believe him now? His one chance to tell her had come and gone. It would just seem like a desperate move by a cornered male. He would tell her, but he was going to do it face to face. So she could look into his face and see his love. So she would know.

He tapped out *Ring me* and hit the send button. He wanted to hurl the ominously silent phone across the room. He wanted to go and get Tabitha out of his bed, put her on a plane and never see her again. He wanted to go back in time and erase that one thoughtless act.

He cursed himself for his own stupidity as he thought back to that day. He had called round to see her to say goodbye on the eve of his departure to Queensland. They'd chatted and she told him about her split from Tony a few weeks previously and he remembered being surprised because he'd really thought she and Tony belonged together. They'd had a beer and a laugh and it had been like old times. Good times. He'd remembered what he had seen in her all those years ago.

And she had kissed him and looked at him with those big eyes and said she couldn't believe he was truly leaving and it was like they were saying their final goodbyes. Finally bringing a close to their relationship. And they'd both been single and it had seemed fitting somehow. But it hadn't seemed so fitting the next morning and they'd both agreed it had been a little foolish.

But their indiscretion had come back to haunt them well and truly. Maddy had looked at him with questioning eyes and the denial that had sprung to his lips had died an instant death. How could he be sure it wasn't his? His mind had crowded with questions as he'd stood mutely trying to comprehend Tab's news.

And then Maddy had left and the enormity of what he'd lost had hit him. Tabitha had tried to talk to him but despite the hundreds of question crowding his mind, Marcus had been so angry he'd known he couldn't get into it with her tonight. Angry at himself—that a moment of weakness and stupidity had hurt Maddy. Hurt the woman he loved.

'It's late, Tab. We'll discuss it in the morning. Have my bed.' He had gone to the linen cupboard pulled out clean sheets, thrust them at her, taken a pillow down for himself and stormed off to the couch, flicking off the light switch as he passed.

And here he lay, his pregnant ex-wife in his bed and the woman he loved gone, refusing to take his calls. He felt impotent and furious at himself and Tabitha for the position they were now in.

He looked at the time on his mobile. Two a.m. He rolled on his side and punched his pillow, squeezing his eyes shut as the heat of his anger burned in his chest. He really needed to get some sleep—tomorrow was going to be harrowing. He and Tabitha had to talk and for that he was going to need all his wits. He forced himself to employ some meditation techniques and forget that for the first day in six weeks he'd be waking up without Maddy.

There were four missed calls and three texts on Madeline's mobile the next morning when she switched it back on. Marcus. She told herself she wasn't going to listen to them, her finger even hovered over the delete button, but a masochistic streak had her dialling her message bank just to hear his voice.

'Maddy, please, Maddy, I'm so sorry. Please, switch your phone back on. Please.'

He sounded bleak and she knew how he felt. It felt like winter inside her again—cold and barren. The warm place inside that he had thawed only a handful of weeks ago snap frozen in a thick block of ice. Had it only been last night she had confessed her feelings? With a sleepless night behind her and her love in tatters, it felt like an age ago. An ice age.

At least his voice hadn't been condescending. He hadn't glibly said he could explain or that there'd been a mistake or dismissed what had happened as nothing. His voice told her how serious the situation was. And she couldn't believe that the happiest six weeks of her life had ended so abruptly.

The questions that had circled her brain endlessly continued. When Tabitha had laid her trump card down she had looked at Marcus, waiting for the denial, waiting for him to dispute what she was saying. But she had seen it in his eyes. The truth. Tabitha's baby was his baby.

And now she was in love with someone who was having a child with another woman. Someone who would be a father to that baby come hell or high water. Someone who obviously still had a thing for his ex-wife. Had he gone straight from Tabitha's bed to hers?

She quashed the urge to cry. And to ring the office and tell Veronica she was ill and couldn't come in today. She would not. She had a day to get through. Patients who relied on her. It wasn't their fault that she was appallingly bad at picking lovers or that Marcus was appallingly bad at keeping his pants on.

And it would give her something else to think about other than the complete shambles her life had become overnight. And Veronica was too damn astute for her own good and she didn't want to face questions she didn't have any answers to.

Marcus gave up on sleep at five-thirty and sat on the deck drinking microwaved coffee from last night's pot, watching the colours of the river change as the sun rose. The morning traffic steadily increased and the River Cats started to ferry their first passengers across the river to their workplaces. His mind churned over and over the events of the night before in all their horrifying detail. He couldn't think of a solution, just more problems.

Tabitha was still asleep when Marcus left for work a couple of hours later. He almost woke her before he left but he remembered how tired being pregnant made her and figured it could wait a bit longer. He had to get to the hospital anyway as he'd promised Jenny Smith he'd call in before work.

He somehow managed to pull an academy-award-winning performance out of thin air. He was bright and breezy and positive because that was what she and Trent needed. But, if anything, seeing Trent look so small and defenceless between the white hospital sheets cemented his conviction. He could never turn his back on his own child.

He tried Maddy's phone again several times before he reached work and hung up when her message bank picked up. Would she ever speak to him again? Did he deserve it? He would keep trying but he didn't know what the hell he would say to her. That he loved her? That they could work it out? How? He didn't have any answers yet.

And he really wouldn't have any until he talked to Tab. There were things he needed to clarify. His head warred with his heart. His head told him he had to do the honourable thing and be with Tabitha and the baby, accept his responsibilities and step up to the plate and be a father. Not one in name only like his own dad, but a hands-on, involved dad.

But his heart said he loved Maddy and any relationship with Tabitha was doomed to failure, even more so than the first time around. If he hadn't had met Maddy he might have been able to fool himself that marrying Tab again could work. But he had.

His mobile rang as he was opening up and his heart leapt. But Tabitha's mobile number was flashing on the screen and he felt his hopes sink.

'Tab,' he said.

'You left without waking me,' she chided.

Marcus wasn't in the mood for pleasantries. 'I had things to do,' he said.

'I was hoping for a grand tour of your new practice,' she said. 'And we need to talk. Do you get to stop for lunch? I could come down then.'

Marcus sighed. The sooner they got this over, the sooner he could figure out what the hell he was going to do. 'One o'clock,' he said, and hit the end button on his phone.

He looked at his watch. Fifteen minutes before his first client. Maddy would be in by now. He rose. He had to see her. If nothing else to apologise. Her wounded eyes from last night haunted him and he wanted to say how very sorry he was that she had been a casualty of Tabitha's announcement. The thought that she was hurt and he had been responsible was more than he could bear.

He stopped at Veronica's desk and gave her his most charming smile. Maddy had teased him mercilessly about the younger woman's adoration and today he wasn't beyond exploiting that. 'I need five minutes of Maddy's time. Can you hold her first patient?' Somehow he managed to smile.

'Too late. She should be finishing soon, though.'

'Can I sneak in before the next one?'

'You've only just left her, Marcus Hunt,' Veronica complained good-naturedly. Maddy's door opened and her patient walked out, holding a script.

'Can you send my next patient in, please, Veronica?'

Even over the intercom Maddy's voice sounded bleak.

'Go on, then,' Veronica said, lowering her voice, 'I can stall for five minutes. Do you want me to announce you?'

Good lord, no! He doubted he'd make it past the desk. 'No, thanks.' He smiled.

'Go get her, tiger.' She growled at him playfully. Marcus left the reception area, feeling a little guilty about misleading Veronica, and approached Maddy's office with great trepidation. She didn't disappoint him. Her reaction was what he'd expected.

She looked up from a chart and saw him standing in the doorway. He looked uncertain. 'Not now, Marcus, I'm busy.' She was proud of how business like she sounded when her heart was breaking.

'Look,' he said as he stepped into the room and shut the door behind him, 'I can—'

'What?' she interrupted. 'Explain? I doubt it.'

'Tabitha—'

'Don't,' she said interrupting again. 'I don't want to hear about whatever little sordid arrangement you've got going.'

'It's not like that,' he denied. She was hurt and lashing out. He would not take it personally.

'So you didn't sleep with her?'

What defence did he have for that? Nothing. It wouldn't matter to Maddy what the circumstances had been or that in the decade of their separation it had been the one and only time. He nodded. 'The night before I left for Queensland.'

The confirmation hit her hard and she bit back a gasp. Even up until now she'd been hoping it had all been a dreadful mistake. She nodded. So, they hadn't been together. He'd been a free agent. But his actions had put their relationship in serious peril. And she wasn't going to hang around and wait for Marcus to choose his ex-wife and their baby over her.

She felt the hot burn of tears in her eyes. 'For God's sake, Marcus, you're a doctor. You should at least have had the brains to have used a condom,' she hissed.

'We did,' he said indignantly. Although they had all those years ago, too, and it hadn't made any difference. Maybe Tabitha's condom supply was suspect?

She stared at him, blinking away the threatening tears. She couldn't do this any more. It hurt too much to think about. 'Just go, Marcus,' she said, refusing to look at him, 'I have a patient.'

'I love you, Maddy.'

She gasped and looked at him incredulously. She felt as if someone had come along with a big stick, swiped her feet out from underneath her and she'd landed flat on her butt. She felt winded.

'What?'

'It's true,' he said calmly.

Madeline let the air whoosh out of her chest in a big huff. She believed him. She could see it all over his face. Oh, now? Now he tells her?

'Oh, right. And when did you have this revelation? Because less than twenty-four hours ago you didn't. I mean, I gave you the perfect opening to tell me last night and you didn't. But suddenly your pregnant ex-wife turns up, and you find the words?'

He knew it would be a hard sell but everything was such a mess right now, he wanted one thing to be right. 'I realised last night when you walked out the door. Tabitha was there and you were gone and it hit me.'

'I didn't notice you running after me down the corridor to tell me.'

'Would it have made a difference at that point?'

She thought about the intensity of her anger and knew she wouldn't have given him the time of day, but she was damned if she was going to let him off the hook. 'Well, I guess we'll never know now, will we?'

'Maddy, please…'

She heard the note of desperation in his voice and could tell he was just as miserable about this turn of events as she was. Despite the mess and her anger and disappointment, she still loved him and could see he was being torn up inside.

She took a deep breath and decided to put him out of his misery. She knew him well enough to know he couldn't walk away from being a father, and when you loved someone you didn't ask them to do things they couldn't do. If she wasn't on the scene this whole situation was going to be so much easier for him. He was so good with children, with Connor and Trent, and he'd make an excellent father. She had to let him go.

'Marcus, go and be with Tabitha and your baby. It's OK—you have my blessing.'

Marcus frowned at her, not quite believing what she was saying. 'I don't want your blessing. I want your love.'

'Well, you can't have it. I take it back. And I never said I loved you anyway. Just that I thought I was falling for you. Luckily for me, Tabitha came along at the right moment.'

'That's rubbish.'

She shrugged. 'I think you have bigger things to think about.'

'But—'

'Just go, Marcus.' *Can't you see my heart is breaking and I'm going to cry any second?* 'I have a patient.'

Thankfully his morning was sufficiently busy to keep his mind off everything. There was so much he hadn't had a chance to say to Maddy. He certainly hadn't believed her when she'd denied loving him. Even if he had to abduct her and tie her to a chair, he would make her listen. But Maddy was right, he had to sort things out with Tab first.

His ex-wife wandered in at one, and stood in his doorway.

'Come in,' he said. 'Sit down.'

Tabitha did as she was asked and looked at Marcus for a few moments. 'I'm sorry about bursting in last night and being rude to your…ah…guest. It was late and I was tired and I guess I just wasn't expecting it. So who is she?'

'Madeline Harrington. She's a GP in the practice next door.'

'It didn't take you long,' she said pleasantly.

'I love her, Tabitha.'

She smiled, unperturbed. 'You used to love me.'

'Oh, Tab, that was forever ago.'

She nodded. 'There is some kind of weird *déjà vu*, though, isn't there? And now we have this second chance.'

He sat back, ignoring the statement. 'Are you sure, Tab?'

She nodded. 'I promise. I did a test. I'm ten weeks.'

Marcus did a quick calculation in his head. That would most certainly fit the time frame. The next question was indelicate to say the least and he hesitated, but it had to be asked.

'How can you be sure it's mine?'

She looked at him sharply. 'Is my word not good enough, Marcus?' she asked quietly.

'Tabitha, please.'

She sighed. 'Because I'd had a period about two weeks before we slept together. And haven't had one since. You were the only person I'd done it with in those two weeks.'

Pretty compelling evidence. 'Have you been to a doctor?'

'I have an appointment with an obstetrician in a month. I was hoping you'd come with me.'

'In Melbourne?'

She nodded and he could see all his hopes and dreams with Maddy and his new practice come crashing down around him.

'I can't move here, Marcus. It's too hot. Too far away from my family and friends.'

So if he wanted a relationship with his baby he was going to have to go back. 'I'm just starting out here,' he said.

'I know but I can't leave Melbourne, Marcus. Please, don't ask me to.'

He nodded, not bothering to disguise the annoyed curl to his lip. But she could ask him to leave everything here? His practice. Maddy. Would Maddy go to Melbourne with him?

'I don't love you.' He didn't mean it to be harsh but everything was so screwed up.

She nodded at him. 'We could make it work this time. For the sake of the baby. This child deserves two parents, Marcus.'

'Yes, thank you, Tabitha. I think I understand that better than anyone.'

'I've booked you a flight home,' she said.

Marcus blinked. 'You what?' he asked quietly.

'You know you'll come.' She shrugged. 'I thought this might make it easier for you.'

There were a lot of things about this situation that he couldn't control but he was damn sure he was going to control the things he could. 'Listen to me very carefully, Tabitha,' he said, his eyes glittering. 'There is plenty of time yet to move, and when and if I do, it will be of my own accord. There are things that need settling here. I can't just take off.'

'You mean you won't,' she said testily.

'I need time.'

'So you can make up with your girlfriend?' she sneered.

'Oh I think you've killed any chance of that.'

'You know I was right. This is just like before. You didn't want a baby then either,' she said bitterly, her voice raising an octave.

'I was twenty-two,' he sighed.

'Well, no need to worry,' she said standing. 'Maybe I'll conveniently miscarry this time again.'

They glared at each other across the desk before Tabitha turned on her heel, storming out of his office. He heard the glass door slide shut with a loud slam.

Two hours later Marcus was seeing a client out when his mobile rang. Again he got his hopes up but again it was just

Tabitha's number that was flashing. He almost didn't answer it, not wishing to get into a slanging match on the phone. But this was as much his fault as hers.

'Hello,' he said tersely.

He couldn't make out a word she said initially she was crying so much. 'Slow down, Tab,' he said, 'I can't understand a word you're saying.'

'I said,' she said hiccuping as she drew in a couple of deep breaths, 'you got your wish, you slimeball. I'm bleeding. I hope you're happy.'

Tabitha dissolved into more tears and Marcus took a few seconds to fully comprehend what she'd said. Oh, no! Not again. Tab had been devastated the first time around, depressed for months after.

'What am I going to do, Marcus?' she wailed. 'I can't go through this again.'

His heart went out to her and his medical training came to the fore. 'What do you mean, bleeding? Fresh blood or more like spotting?' he asked.

'Spotting.' She sniffled.

'Any cramping?'

'Not yet.' Her voice wobbled.

'It's probably nothing, Tab,' he said reassuringly.

'This was how it started last time,' she sobbed.

'Come down here immediately,' he said. 'They have a basic ultrasound unit next door, we'll do a scan and see what's happening.'

Marcus made some phone calls. Three to cancel all his remaining afternoon clients and one more to Maddy, who thankfully picked it up without looking at her caller ID.

'I know this is asking a lot but Tabitha is spotting. She's hysterical. Can I bring her in for a quick scan?'

Madeline couldn't quite believe what he was asking of her. She wanted to scream into the phone and hang up loudly in his ear. But despite everything, Madeline felt for Tabitha. Many of her patients had suffered from the devastating loss of a pregnancy. It was only natural for Marcus to turn to the most readily available source of medical equipment.

'Of course,' she said politely. 'Is she cramping?'

'No.'

'How far is she along? It's probably nothing,' she said to him unnecessarily.

'I know, that's what I told her, but she's been through this once before. She's ten weeks. She's really upset, Maddy.'

She heard the apology and the strain in his voice and hardened herself against it. 'Bring her straight in,' she said briskly, and hung up.

Once her hands had stopped shaking and she could think rationally, she hoped for Tabitha's sake everything was OK. And she was glad that Marcus had asked her. This way she got to see the baby, too, and it would seem much more real to her than it did at the moment. Everything from last night onward seemed surreal. Seeing Marcus's baby on the screen, while devastating, would also help to make it real. Confirm that it was actually happening—that he had responsibilities and she wouldn't stand in his way.

Madeline maintained her professional veneer as she ushered the man that she loved and the woman he had im-pregnated into the examination room where the small, rather old ultrasound machine lived.

Tabitha, her eyes red-rimmed, got up on the couch and pulled her skirt down a little to reveal her still flat stomach. Madeline ignored Marcus, who looked miserable, not wanting to feel any kind of empathy for him at the moment.

She switched the machine on and noticed how Tabitha reached for his hand and he automatically took it. 'You've been spotting?' Madeline asked. She needed to say something to stop the roar of blood in her head. Watching their easy familiarity was torture.

'It started an hour ago.'

'And what were you doing at the time?' she asked, pretending that this was just another client as she palpated Tabitha's abdomen. She could easily feel the bulge of the burgeoning uterus and frowned slightly. At ten weeks she shouldn't be able to feel the uterine fundus yet. It didn't grow up from behind the pelvic rim until about twelve weeks.

'Marcus and I had had an argument. I was crying,' she said.

Madeline looked at Marcus and she saw the guilt on his face. Her heart swelled with love. Damn it. And damn him. Here she was, caught up in a bizarre triangle with the absolute right to feel like the most injured party, and all she wanted to do was take him in her arms and comfort him.

'And have you been taking care of yourself?' she asked. 'Eating well, sleeping well?'

'I had my best night's sleep in a long time,' Tabitha sniffled. 'I've always slept best in Marcus's bed.'

Marcus gaped at Tabitha as he watched Maddy's reaction. She covered it swiftly but he could see his ex-wife's barb had hit hard. It was unlike Tabitha to be so cruel. There was something going on that she wasn't telling him.

He clenched his fists. 'I slept on the couch,' he said tersely, looking at Maddy, relieved to see her shoulders relax.

Madeline squeezed some gel onto Tabitha's abdomen and felt a guilty pleasure in the woman's swift intake of breath as the cold goo hit her skin. Normally she would warn the patient first. It wasn't very professional of her but Tabitha's last dig had hit its mark and it had stung.

The screen was quite small, about ten centimetres square, but as Madeline ran the transducer through the gel the image of a very healthy-looking foetus flickered on the screen. The heart beat strongly and nothing appeared irregular or out of place. If Tabitha had been in the early stages of miscarrying, Madeline would have expected to find an abnormality with the foetus itself—an irregularity in the sac or more probably no heartbeat.

Madeline's suspicions were confirmed, however. No way was this a ten-week pregnancy. She'd guess it to be closer to fourteen weeks, definitely second trimester. She knew that the machine would give her an actual gestation at the end but wondered if Marcus had picked it up.

'The baby looks fine. It has a very strong heartbeat,' Madeline said to Tabitha.

She sneaked a peak at Marcus and wished she hadn't. The look of wonder on his face made her feel physically ill. She could see the usual reactions when people saw their babies for the first time and she knew it was all over between them.

She felt irrational tears spring to her eyes and a rising surge of jealousy. How would it feel to have Marcus's baby inside *her?* To have him look at *their* baby like that? Like it was the most precious thing he had ever seen. The yearning was intense and she almost wished she was pregnant herself. At least she would be able to take a little of Marcus away from this mess and she'd never be alone again.

Marcus was totally caught up in the image on the screen. He remembered seeing the twelve-week ultrasound pictures of the baby Tabitha had miscarried years ago and clearly remembered not feeling anything other than a sinking sense of dread.

He hadn't seen the fuzzy images as the wonder and awe

of new life but a representation of the end of his life as he'd known it. But right now he felt a weird connection with the strong yet fragile new life. His baby's heartbeat blinked rapidly at him and he felt a primal urge to protect it from anything that could harm it.

Since when had he felt like this about a baby? He certainly hadn't felt it all those years ago. He looked up and saw Maddy staring at him with glassy eyes. Since falling in love and wanting it all with her. There was only one thing wrong with this picture—the baby was in the wrong womb.

If only he had that magic wand Maddy had accused him of having at their first acquaintance. Looking at the baby and feeling his love for it rising in his chest, he realised everything would have been perfect had it only been inside Maddy—the woman he loved.

He knew in that instant if this mess was ever sorted out and he could convince Maddy to take him back, having their own baby was a must. He wanted to see their baby on a screen. And growing inside her and coming into the world and being cuddled into her breast. He wanted it so badly it hurt.

And then he realised that there was something else wrong with the picture. He'd been so caught up in the image and the unexpected rush of love that he hadn't seen the most obvious thing. He looked at Madeline and he knew that she had spotted it, too.

'What's the gestation?' he asked her.

Madeline's hand shook as she pressed the button, fully aware that Marcus had seen the discrepancy. 'Fifteen weeks one day,' she read off the screen.

Marcus felt a virtual storm of emotions. 'It's not mine?' he muttered to her.

Madeline shook, overwhelming relief temporarily overriding her hurt and anger.

'What? No, that's impossible,' said Tabitha, rising up onto her elbows.

'I'm afraid it is,' said Madeline.

And Tabitha lay back and burst into tears.

CHAPTER TEN

MADELINE made a huge show of unplugging the machine and cleaning up as Marcus stood beside Tabitha, comforting her.

'I'm…so…sorry,' Tabitha faltered out between huge body-racking sobs. 'Please don't…hate me… I'm so…sorry.'

'Come on, Tab. Stop crying.' He wiped the goo off her tummy gently and pulled her shirt down. There was obviously more to this story. 'Sit up, dry your face and tell me.'

Tabitha did as he asked and Madeline handed him a box of tissues as she pushed the machine towards the door. They obviously needed to talk and they didn't need her hanging around in the background. She had been watching their interaction, their casual intimacy with a sick fascination. She had wanted to run from the room but her body was reacting sluggishly, almost in slow motion, to the frantic get-out signals from her brain.

'I have a patient to get back to. I'll let Marcus see you out,' she said as she opened the door.

'Wait, Maddy,' Marcus said.

Madeline shook her head at him and looked at him through watery eyes. 'I have to get back,' she said, and turned on her heel and fled.

Marcus wanted to go to her. She looked miserable and he

knew that performing the ultrasound must have been very difficult for her. But whether he liked it or not, his ex-wife took precedence.

He thrust a glass of water at Tabitha. 'Talk,' he said to her when her sobs had slowly dried up to the odd hiccup.

'It's Tony's,' she said, staring into the glass of water. 'That's why he left me. I told him I was pregnant and he freaked.'

'Why?' Marcus could understand a twenty-two-year-old freaking but a mid-thirties white-collar worker?

'Something about not having a clue about kids. I think he just panicked, it wasn't like we'd planned it or anything. And then you came along that night and I thought maybe if I got back with you then Tony would be jealous and realise that he couldn't live without me. Or the baby.'

Marcus couldn't believe it. 'Hell, Tab. What the hell were you thinking? This isn't like you.'

'I know, I'm sorry, I was desperate. I know how you feel about fatherless kids and, well…you'd married me once before for the sake of a baby.'

'How long did you plan on keeping this charade up for? Would you really have let me marry you?'

'Would you have?' she asked.

He looked at her for a moment. 'I don't know, Tab. Maybe.'

'I wouldn't have let you marry me.'

Well, thanks heaven for small mercies. 'You were just going to manipulate me for a little while longer?'

'Oh, God, it sounds so callous, I know. I love him, Marcus. I just wasn't thinking straight. I'm sorry. I had no right to involve you.'

'Damn right!' Marcus paced around the room. 'Give me one good reason why I shouldn't put you over my knee and tan your backside? Hell, Tab, have you any idea what you've done?'

'Maddy.' Tabitha nodded. 'I've ruined it for you, haven't I?'

'I sincerely hope not,' he said, running a hand through his hair. 'But you sure as hell have muddied the waters.'

'She seems nice,' said Tabitha.

'She is, Tab. She's the best thing that's happened to me in years.'

'I'm sorry I've interfered in your life. It's unforgivable.'

'You know you just could have asked me to talk to Tony or something. Since when have I ever knocked you back?'

'I know. I just felt so foolish, being in the same tight spot all over again. Maybe it's hormones. It seemed like a really good plan at the time. I just hadn't factored in Maddy or your feelings for her.' The tears started again. 'What can I do to fix it?'

Marcus stopped pacing, alarmed. 'Oh, God, Tab. I think you've done more than enough! Just go back to Melbourne and stay the hell out of it.'

'OK, OK.' She held her hands up.

There was silence in the room for a few minutes while Marcus paced and Tabitha watched him, feeling wretched.

'Madeline's the one, isn't she?'

He stopped pacing. 'Yes, she is.'

'Well, what are you waiting for? Tell her your ex-wife is a manipulative, conniving bitch. Tell her I'm unbalanced. Tell her I'm sorry. Tell her whatever it takes but just go and get her back.'

Marcus knocked gently on Madeline's office door and then opened it slowly. He knew she was alone because a very cautious Veronica had told him so.

'Something's wrong, Marcus,' she'd said, eyeing him suspiciously. 'I don't know what it is.'

He'd patted her hand. 'It's OK. I think I do.'

'Have you two had your first tiff?'

Now, there was an understatement. 'Something like that,' he'd said.

Veronica had stood, leaned across the desk pulled him down by the scruff of his shirt until they had been eye to eye. 'You hurt her and I'll kill you.' He'd believed her.

Madeline looked up at the knock to see Marcus standing in her doorway. She'd been having a good cry and knew she must look a mess. She sat up straight, pulled a tissue out of the box on her desk and blew her nose.

She looked so distant and he felt completely lost. He could see he was losing her. 'Please, Maddy. Tell me what to say to make it better. I don't know what to say,' he said, his arms aching to hold her.

'Well, that makes two of us,' she said.

'For God's sake,' he said, desperation making him angry, 'the baby's not even mine.'

'No, but you wanted it to be. You wanted that baby—I saw it in your face.'

A denial rose to his lips but he thought better of it. Seeing the baby on the screen had definitely switched on his paternal instinct. For a second, blocking out all the convoluted mess of the last twelve hours, he had wanted the baby. But he'd wanted it to be theirs. His and Maddy's. Not his and Tabitha's.

He saw the two red spots of colour in her cheeks and how the shine of tears emphasised the deep rich glitter in her emerald eyes. And knowing he was responsible was killing him.

'You're right. I had a revelation when I saw that baby on the screen that really pulled me up. I realised that after years of not wanting one that I did want a baby. That I wanted to be a father, very much. I've never felt that way. Never. And it's because of you. Loving you makes me want things I've never wanted before. I wanted it to be *our* baby on that ultrasound screen. Yours and mine.'

Madeline swallowed hard. His voice was husky with passion. The plea in his voice unmistakable. She let herself think about having his child inside her for a moment. A part of him. A family of her own. It had been so long since she'd been part of a family.

He sounded genuine and despite the dictates of her sensible brain, her heart was flowering, his earlier declaration of love and his admission that he wanted to have babies with her like welcome rain nourishing fragile petals. She felt the bloom swelling in her chest and she wanted to have the chance to nurture it.

But at the same time her brain urged retreat. How could she put her heart out there again? She'd taken a risk with him and his heat and his passion had warmed her all the way through and it had been fantastic while it had lasted. But the ending had been awful and she just couldn't trust him with her heart again.

How could she knowingly get involved with someone still so heavily caught up with his ex-wife? Sex with the ex might be a hip thing to do these days but she couldn't live like that. How could she trust that he wouldn't succumb again?

'And what happens when Tabitha turns up our doorstep one day and you end up in bed together?'

Marcus blinked. Did she really think he would cheat on her? He felt angry that she would even think that of him. 'What?'

'Well, you've obviously had problems in the past, realising you're divorced,' she pointed out, trying to stay calm.

'Let's get this straight,' he said, beginning to realise the damage Tabitha had done to Madeline's trust. He should have tanned her hide after all! 'What happened between Tab and I was incredibly stupid but I'm not going to apologise for it. I'm sorrier than you can know that you got caught up in the consequences but we were both single and free to sleep with whoever we wanted, including each other. And in the ten years since our divorce it was the only time it ever happened.'

'How do I know it won't happen again?'

'Because I don't cheat, Maddy. Never.'

She so wanted to believe him. 'But she's very attractive.'

'Listen to me,' he said, crouching in front of her. 'I don't love her, I don't want her. I only ever want to be with you.'

She looked into his earnest blue eyes and wanted to believe him, but the scene from last night kept replaying in her head and she didn't want to trust her heart to him and be back in this position ever again. She sat back in her chair, distancing herself from his presence. Her temples were starting to throb. 'I don't know, Marcus. Too much has happened. I can't think properly.'

He stood, bitterly disappointed that she hadn't taken him at his word. 'You shouldn't have to think,' he said calmly, trying to be rational. 'You should know. We've been inseparable for six weeks. You should know in your gut. Trust your gut, Maddy.'

Just like a man to simplify the emotion out of it. She shook her head and swallowed the threatening tears. He didn't get to tell her what she should know. 'The only thing I know in my gut at the moment is that the man who supposedly loves me is still sexually attracted to his ex-wife.'

Marcus felt like she'd hit him with a hammer between the

eyes. How could he convince her that he felt nothing for Tabitha? 'It wasn't like that, Maddy. It was a spur-of-the-moment thing.'

'And when another moment comes along?'

He sighed, seeing the confusion in her eyes. She looked utterly torn. Too much had happened and they weren't getting anywhere by going back over the same ground.

'I love you, Maddy, and I know you love me, too. We can make this work. Don't shut me out.'

'I can't. You're asking too much of me. Everyone I've loved has left me or let me down. My parents. Abby. Simon. And now you. I should have kept that damn ring on and pretended my life was fine.'

Marcus was horrified at the very thought. 'Oh, no, Maddy. You were so shut off, so guarded. You can't seriously want to go back there.'

'Yes,' she said, nodding her head vigorously, tears streaming down her face. 'Because I know how to play that role. There's two roles I know how to play really well in my life. One is the shut-off Madeline and the other is the grieving Madeline. And I know which hurts less.'

'Maddy, no,' he said, reaching for her.

'Get out,' she said on a sob. 'Just go. Please, go.'

He opened his mouth to object but he had upset her again and each tear was like a drop of acid searing his flesh. She looked so miserable and it tore at his insides.

Madeline watched him walk out, staring after him, wanting to call him back but too confused to trust her gut like he'd asked her to do. Her brain hurt. The throb was developing into a migraine. And Marcus wouldn't be around to massage this one away. She pulled out another tissue from the box as her face crumpled.

* * *

She was about to finish for the day when Veronica buzzed her.

'There's a Tabitha here to see you,' she said.

Madeline paused. What the—? Her headache had built steadily, the two tablets she had taken at lunch just managing to hold it in check. Did she really want to confront the woman who had given her the damn thing in the first place?

'Send her in,' she said, too weary to think. How much more emotionally draining could this day get?

Tabitha entered and, despite Marcus's assurances that Tabitha and he were long over, Madeline felt an unreasonable streak of jealousy.

'Sit down.' She indicated the chair to the other woman.

'I owe you an apology,' Tabitha said, sitting. 'Last night was unforgivable.'

Madeline looked at her hands, not saying anything. Last night had replayed in her head so much she was giddy with it.

'I didn't expect to see Marcus with a woman. You see, I had this plan to carry out and you well and truly threw a spanner in the works.'

'Oh?' Madeline asked, her curiosity piqued despite the pounding of her head. She listened as Tabitha told her all about it and by the end she even felt sorry for Marcus.

'So what are you going to do now?' Madeline asked.

'Marcus phoned Tony and spoke to him. I owe him big time for that, which is why I'm here. He didn't have to help me after the stunt I pulled. I'm surprised he hasn't strangled me. Mind you, he probably will if he ever finds out I'm here. But I'm flying out soon.' She stopped, suddenly looking worried. 'That's all right, isn't it? You said the baby's OK? Everything looked good, right?'

'Yes. The foetus looked very healthy. Just rest for the nex* couple of days. If the spotting continues or gets heavier or you experience any cramping, go and see your GP,' Madeline advised. It felt surreal to be calmly advising Tabitha like she was just any patient.

'I will.' The other woman nodded. 'I'm keen to get back and see Tony and start sorting out our problems.'

'Good for you,' said Madeline with a tight smile. Chit-chat after all that had happened between them seemed so trite.

'Marcus is in love with you.'

'Apparently, yes.'

Tabitha waited for a few seconds for Madeline to elaborate. 'You don't understand. Marcus had never been in love with anyone. Not even me, really.'

'And yet he slept with you.'

Tabitha nodded, regarding Madeline closely. 'Marcus told me you were having problems with that. Please, let me assure you, that wasn't about love. That was part of my grand plan to get Tony back. And as far as Marcus was concerned, it was just a pleasant way to say goodbye. Don't punish him for something that happened before he even met you.'

'Except it had huge consequences for Marcus and I, didn't it?' Madeline said testily. 'I don't mean to be rude but to quote a famous person, there are three people in this relationship. And I'm sorry, that's just not going to work for me.'

'I don't blame you. I'm sorry I've stuffed everything up for both of you. I hope you guys work it out. I like you. You're good for him.'

'You don't even know me,' Madeline said, not really warmed by Tabitha's faith.

'I know you ultrasounded me when you must have felt like scratching my eyes out. I know I left a broken-hearted man just now. I know he wants a baby with you that he never wanted with me.'

Madeline said nothing, her head pounding with the migraine and the heaviness of her thoughts.

Tabitha stood. 'I'm on my way to the airport. Please, please, give Marcus another chance. And maybe one day you and I can become friends.' She put out her hand.

Madeline stood and clasped Tabitha's hand automatically, her good manners coming to the fore. Friends? Her head throbbed at the thought.

A week went by. It was hell. Madeline kept on going over and over the same stuff. He loved her. She loved him. Tabitha was out of the picture. What was the problem? Was she punishing him? Was she punishing herself for jumping in and blurring the line between rebound sex and love so quickly?

He sent flowers. He rang. He texted. She just felt numb. Another person she had let in enough to love and he had left her, too. Only it was so much harder this time round to be alone because she had loved him so intensely in their brief time together and knowing he wanted to have a baby with her was torture. She wove fantasies in her head during the long, long nights about her and Marcus being together, getting married, setting up house together. Having a baby. Having two. Three. Making a family together.

She went through the motions of life. Her colleagues were very kind and supportive but also very worried. It was Veronica who got her through the days. She brought her coffee and snacks between patients and insisted that Madeline eat them. She fussed around like a mother hen and entertained her via the intercom with readings from a book called *One hundred and one ways to murder your ex*.

But life was suddenly so bleak and she rued the day she'd ever met Marcus.

A week later Madeline was at the hospital at two in the morning. She'd been called to a terminally ill patient's house because his condition had worsened and his exhausted family hadn't been able to cope any longer. She'd called an ambulance and accompanied the patient to the palliative care ward.

She yawned as she shut the patient's chart and placed it back in the trolley.

'Madeline?'

'Simon! It's so good to see you.' And it was. It had been two months since she'd seen him. He was in scrubs and looked as tired as she felt. He held out his arms and she accepted his hug.

'What brings you to this neck of the woods at such an ungodly hour?' he asked, pulling out of the embrace.

She filled him in and they chatted for a little while catching up on each other's lives. Madeline had expected their first meeting to be awkward but it was just like old times. Two good friends having a chinwag. It was nice but she couldn't quite believe as they talked that she'd ever thought herself in love with him.

'What about your love life?' she asked.

Simon blushed. 'I have met someone. Her name's Marcia. She's fantastic. I'm going to ask her to marry me.'

Madeline blinked but she could see his excitement. 'That's great, Simon, really great. I'm happy for you.'

He laughed. 'I thought you were going to give me a hard time about rushing it.'

'Well, I suppose, given your track record, I'm a little surprised,' she teased. 'You haven't, have you?'

'No way. This is so right it's scary.'

She felt tears prick her eyes. 'How do you know, Simon?'

'I knew from the moment I saw her.'

'But how do you know it's going to work?'

He sighed. 'I don't, Madeline, there are no absolute guarantees. After our, er, prolonged…relationship, I just know life's too short to second-guess everything. I don't want to go another ten years of my life being too cautious to live a little. And if it all falls in a heap, at least I'll have been happy for a while. She's the one, Madeline. I know it in here.' He patted his chest. 'You've just got to trust your gut.'

Trust her gut. She walked out to the car park with those words still in her head. Trust her gut. The same words Marcus had used. What did her gut say? Remove what had happened and Tabitha and the baby—what was her gut telling her about Marcus?

She sat in the car for ages, peeling away the layers of her hurt and all the stuff that had muddied the waters between them. Her gut told her—he was the one. She smiled and then she grinned and then she laughed. Marcus Hunt was the one!

She revved the engine and accelerated away from the hospital. Her heart was pounding, her mind clearer than it had ever been. She'd been so foolish! She hoped it wasn't too late.

She was slightly breathless when she banged on Marcus's door twelve minutes later. She wanted to yell at him to hurry and stood there in an awful panic, hoping that he hadn't already found someone to replace her. What if he was having rebound sex right now?

Suddenly she felt ill and was just about to turn and go when the door opened. He looked haggard and unshaven and delicious and any doubts she had vanished. He was her guy—

her life was incomplete without him. She burst into tears and walked straight into his arms.

'I'm so sorry,' she blubbered. 'I've been so stupid.'

Marcus held her tight, his surprise replaced by an overwhelming sense of relief and love. 'Maddy, oh, thank God, Maddy.' He snaked his fingers into her glorious loose hair and held her to him as she sobbed.

'I was foolish and jealous,' she said, pulling back from his shoulder and wiping the tears away with her hand. 'I never should have doubted you. I was angry at you and punished you for something that had happened before we met. I'm sorry. Please, forgive me. You've pulled me out of this terrible limbo I was in and helped me to live again. And now everything sucks so badly. I don't want to live another moment without you in my life.'

'Maddy, Maddy, Maddy,' he said, cradling her face as he rained kisses all over it. 'I love you. This last fortnight has been hell. I'm sorry my actions hurt you. I never wanted that to happen. Can you ever forgive me? You do know you're the only woman for me, right?'

She kissed him then. A long deep kiss that said it better than words ever could. He picked her up and kicked the door shut behind them.

'I'm never letting you out of my sight again,' he said when her feet touched down seconds later on his bedroom floor. 'Let's get married.'

Madeline laughed, giddy with delight. 'On one condition.'

'What,' he asked kissing down her neck.

'Let's not wait ten years to do it.'

'Ten years?' He gave her a hard, possessive kiss. 'I don't even want to wait ten minutes.'

And they tumbled backwards onto the bed.

4 Books
and a surprise gift!

We would like to take this opportunity to thank you for reading this Mills & Boon® book by offering you the chance to take FOUR more specially selected titles from the Medical Romance™ series absolutely FREE! We're also making this offer to introduce you to the benefits of the Mills & Boon® Reader Service™—

- ★ FREE home delivery
- ★ FREE gifts and competitions
- ★ FREE monthly Newsletter
- ★ Exclusive Reader Service offers
- ★ Books available before they're in the shops

Accepting these FREE books and gift places you under no obligation to buy, you may cancel at any time, even after receiving your free shipment. Simply complete your details below and return the entire page to the address below. You don't even need a stamp!

YES! Please send me 4 free Medical Romance books and a surprise gift. I understand that unless you hear from me, I will receive 6 superb new titles every month for just £2.89 each, postage and packing free. I am under no obligation to purchase any books and may cancel my subscription at any time. The free books and gift will be mine to keep in any case.

M7ZEF

Ms/Mrs/Miss/Mr ....Initials ....
BLOCK CAPITALS PLEASE
Surname ....
Address ....

....

....Postcode ....

Send this whole page to:
UK: FREEPOST CN81, Croydon, CR9 3WZ